GRATEFULLY DEAD

Ghosts of Carrington
Book 3

Maddie James

Sand Dune Books

GRATEFULLY DEAD

Ghosts of Carrington, Book 3

Maddie James

Maddie's VIP Insider News

Be the first to get the news about my books—new releases, free ebooks, sales and discounts, sneak peeks, and exclusive content! Just add your email address at this link: https://maddiejamesbooks.com/pages/newsletter

Gratefully Dead

Ghosts of Carrington, Book 3

One more deadly romantic comedy. *Meet Mitzi, Molly, and Marla—three sisters, southern-fried born-and-bred, and the ghosts who love them.*

Marla Newberry has no interest in dating someone local. She much prefers midnight runs to a biker bar in Shreveport.

Cooter Haines, drummer for a Grateful Dead tribute band called Skull Bone, owns the biker bar called The Deadhead. He also happens to be the only guy who can curl her toes like a sprung guitar string. And while she enjoys surrendering to his toe-curling on occasion, she's not interested in bringing the long-haired drummer home to daddy—until the night Cooter tells her he loves her, and then comes up missing.

That Saturday night, a rival drummer makes a deal with the devil (aka the Skull Bone's manager) and steals the drummer job away from Cooter. Cooter angrily speeds off on his bike and doesn't return. Marla smells a rat.

Later, she wakes up to find a ghostly Cooter sitting at the

foot of her bed. Dead isn't so great, he tells her, and those rumors about Southern Rock bands jamming in Heaven? He's seen no evidence. Plus, he's pretty sure someone jacked up something on his Harley making him roll the bike. He needs her help to find out who wanted him dead.

But is Cooter really dead, or was Marla only dreaming? And days later, where is he?

Can she and her sisters solve this final mystery of the men in their lives, and the ghosts(?) who love them?

Chapter One

Marla Newberry glanced up from her coffee and stared at the yellowed plastic clock on the diner wall. The place smelled of bacon grease, coffee, and the lingering aftermath of someone's flowery perfume. The counter was empty at this hour, most folks having cleared out after the Saturday morning breakfast rush.

The old clock ticked steadily, its hands sweeping the face in unbroken movement.

Tick. Tick. Tick.

Her sisters sat huddled in a corner booth a few feet away, speaking in hushed tones. She'd avoided them ever since they had arrived. Sighing, she ran a hand through her hair and sat up straighter. They were talking about her.

"Give it up, ladies," she called out.

Mitzi smirked. "What?"

"You know."

Molly twisted in her seat. "You gonna mope all day or join us?" Her bright blue eyes flashed with the challenge of her words. Molly was the youngest of the three sisters and never at a loss for words.

Marla stood, smoothing the wrinkles from her faded jeans. "I'm not moping." She lifted her cup and saucer. She loved that the diner used old-fashioned cups and saucers rather than mugs. "You've been staring into your coffee for an hour," Mitzi added. "Surprised you even saw us come in. Get over here. We were just talking about the Halloween festival next month. Help us plan."

Ah yes, the annual small town, Carrington, Louisiana Halloween Festival. Her family had volunteered for years, and this year would be no different. Marla slid into the booth beside Mitzi, her middle sister.

Mitzi's eyes showed concern, and Marla felt a pang of guilt. Her sisters worried too much.

"Plenty of time for festival planning, you know. I'm sure Mom's on it."

"She is, of course," Molly said. "Dad's doing the dunking booth again."

Of course. Dad loved that thing.

"It is September, you know. October is just around the corner," Mitzi added.

"I know that. School just started." She definitely knew school had started because she was teaching English this year, and her middle schoolers were already kicking her butt.

"Three weeks ago." Molly sipped her coffee. "Ewe. This is cold." She signaled the server behind the counter.

Mitzi widened her eyes, looking directly at Marla. "Distracted much?" She waited for a response, sipping from the straw in her chocolate shake, her cheeks sucking in. "You were lost in thought over there."

"I'm fine. Just lesson planning in my head. I have a job, you know."

Molly snorted. "Nice try. We know you've been thinking about Cooter."

The server came and refilled their coffee cups. Heat rose in Marla's cheeks at the mention of his name. When the young woman left, she said, "I don't know what you mean."

"Oh please," Mitzi scoffed. "You've been wandering around with that confused and pained look on your face for a couple of months now. Ever since you two—"

"Can we talk about something else?" Marla interrupted sharply. She didn't want to think or talk about Cooter Haines or the memory of his lips on hers, warm and tasting of whiskey.

Molly and Mitzi exchanged a glance, then Mitzi squeezed Marla's hand. "Of course. Whatever you want."

The old clock continued its steady beat.

Tick. Tick. Tick.

The sound was barely audible above the din of the traffic outside and voices in the diner, and most people probably didn't even hear it. But she did. Why was she so focused on it?

Was time running out? For what?

Her heart, however, beat anything but steady. She stared into her coffee again, wishing for the familiar comfort of routine. But since the random and impromptu and decadent and subsequently repetitive encounters with Cooter started a few months ago, nothing was routine anymore.

It wasn't like her to be so enamored of a man that he occupied her every living and breathing moment, every thought in her brain. She was more of a love 'em and leave 'em kind of girl. Er, woman. She and Cooter had shared a warm and friendly relationship for a couple of years—it had always been hands and lips off—until it wasn't.

Until about six months ago.

Tick. Tick. Tick.

At first it had been delicious fun—scrambling off to the storeroom in the back or sneaking up to his apartment over the bar. Neither of them had talked about anything more than an occasional toe-touching romp—easing the tension of the week and having a little whisky-induced fun.

Until the last time, a couple of months ago, and Cooter had gotten serious.

So serious, in fact, he'd mentioned the L-word.

Marla wasn't ready for the L-word. She made that quite clear that night.

She'd not seen him since.

It wasn't him.

It was her.

Tick. Tick. Tick.

Mitzi patted the table in front of Marla. "Earth to sister. Earth to sister. Goodness, that man has you all swoony and everything."

Shaking herself, Marla stuck out her tongue. "Does not." She glanced once more at the clock on the wall, then refused to think about it. Time with Cooter? Running out? Ridiculous.

"Whatever. Hey. I was thinking of going out tonight. Hubby is in New Orleans on business. Want to go to Shreveport?"

Molly grinned. "I do. Brody is off work tonight. I could see him."

"Good. He hangs out at Deadhead, right?" Mitzi then focused on Marla. "You're coming too. No excuse."

Deadhead was Cooter's bar. Marla shook her head. "No. I've... I have other plans."

Mitzi dismissed that. "I think Skull Bone is playing there tonight. Do you know for sure?"

What the heck was she getting at? Cooter was the drummer for Skull Bone, a Grateful Dead tribute band. He was super awesome with the sticks, one of the best drummers around. They played Deadhead often, so it wasn't really a big deal. Shrugging, she said, "More than likely."

"Then go with us."

She shook her head. "No. Plans, remember?"

Tick. Tick. Tick.

Damn it. Stop.

Molly gestured with a hand. "Oh, pooh. Change them."

She shouldn't. But she kind of wanted to. "I don't know. I have to think about it. Call you later?"

Mitzi stood, grabbing the check. "Just make sure you do, sister. Don't give us the slip. We'll be there by nine."

Marla nodded. "Fine."

Looking proud and pleased, Mitzi's grin widened. "I'm picking up your coffee, too. See you later."

Marla watched them leave. They'd done it to her again.

* * *

Late in the afternoon, Marla went for a hike at Kisatchie National Forest to clear her head, and to keep her from thinking about Cooter and going to Shreveport and the biker bar. She'd willed herself to stop thinking about ticking clocks and time running out. That was all weird, anyway—that old clock.

Instead, she simply wanted to clear her brain and get some exercise to tire out her body.

She could have ridden her bike, her Harley—it was a beautiful afternoon for it—but decided instead to take the jeep. The hike would exhaust her. She didn't need to ride home on the bike.

Exhaustion was perhaps what she needed right now. She'd not slept well lately and could use a good night's sleep.

The worn trail stretched before her as she made her way into the woods, sunlight filtering through the canopy above. The sun streamed through the trees, creating a shifting, shimmering layer of light and shadow. Her boots crunched on the pine needle-strewn path, a soothing rhythm that calmed her soul somewhat.

Outside of a warbling bird and an occasional squirrel's chatter, the forest was quiet—and she felt at peace. She could lose herself in the winding trails and the solitude.

She quickened her pace. The trail sloped upwards, straining her muscles, and she savored the burn in her thighs. It had been a while since she'd had a good physical workout. Fatigue quieted her restless mind, and for a while she thought of nothing but the terrain ahead.

Nothing like a long hike to put things into perspective.

By the time she returned to her Jeep, dusk had crept into daylight. She drove back toward Carrington with the windows down; the air scented with pine and promise. After about an hour of driving and musing, she realized she was at a crossroads.

Literally.

Turn left to go to Carrington and home. Right would take her to Shreveport and The Deadhead.

Impulsively, she turned toward Shreveport.

Damn it. Was this a mistake?

She drove on.

Some nights the stars shone so brightly they lit the country road, but tonight clouds obscured the sky. Marla wondered if that was an omen of doom. What would Cooter think, her showing up again? Now?

An hour later, she pulled into the gravel lot of The Deadhead.

Neon signs glowed in the dimness, advertising Lone Star beer and Jim Beam. From within came the familiar strains of "Friend of the Devil," a frequently played Grateful Dead song at the bar.

Marla gripped the steering wheel, her heart pounding.

The Deadhead biker bar sat near the end of town, in a

secluded area. Cooter had told her once that when he bought the place, and told others he was opening a bar there, that they laughed. It was too far out of town, they said. No one would come all the way out there for a beer.

But Cooter thought otherwise and persevered. They came for the beer, the atmosphere, and the music. And they came often.

The loud music and revved up bikes didn't bother anyone, which was a good thing, because both were loud and often. She hadn't been to Deadhead in weeks, avoiding the surge of longing and desire Cooter's presence evoked. But tonight, the lure of music and memory proved too strong.

Tick. Tick. Tick.

"Oh, stop it. Damn it! I'm going."

Looking down at herself, still dressed in hiking shorts and a T-shirt, desperately needing a shower, and shook her head. Not bar clothes, that was for certain. Not that the patrons of The Deadhead really cared.

Which they didn't.

She got out of the Jeep and walked to the entrance, pushing open the creaking wooden door. The smoky interior was crowded, as always, bikers and locals mingling over pool tables and beers.

Marla sighed, glancing around the dimly lit interior. She loved the atmosphere, the live music and cold beer—she was more than ready for a cold one, to be honest.

She'd long ago decided she preferred the untamed atmosphere of The Deadhead, having grown tired of the safe, quaint, and predictable, small-town scene in Carrington. The men there were fine for happily-ever-after, but she was more of a casual fling woman. No man she'd ever met in Carrington shared her thirst for adventure or understood her free spirit.

And as a teacher, she also couldn't afford any gossip or

drama. Her students would have a field day if they saw her out with a different man every weekend. Middle school kids were the worst. It was simpler to avoid local dating altogether.

She wasn't fond of the music row bar scene near the river in downtown Shreveport, either. A bit on the seedier side of life, she'd braved it when she was younger and with a group of her girlfriends. Bar hopping was a thing back then, right out of college. But now, Cooter's place was where she wanted to be, for the beer, an occasional whiskey sour, and of course, Cooter.

Marla's gaze drifted to the leather-topped bar. A crowd of men and women huddled up against it. She'd met Cooter sitting at that bar two years ago and had bonded instantly over their mutual love of the Grateful Dead and motorcycle road trips.

While Marla cherished her independence, she couldn't deny the connection between them. Cooter was a talented drummer, and she loved the music. He owned a bar, and she liked beer and whiskey. Like Marla, he had a Harley and craved the freedom and new experiences the open road offered.

When she was with Cooter, her heart raced with excitement and possibility.

And there. There he was, standing behind the bar—tall and rugged in worn jeans and a leather vest, pushing his shoulder-length and graying hair away from his face, while drawing beers from the tap, and talking up the customers.

Cooter. Her Cooter?

Marla stood frozen in place, caught between leaving and rushing into his arms. Their last encounter had been bitter and painful, a clash of stubborn wills that left her aching with loss. But one look at Cooter, and she knew nothing had really changed. Her heart belonged to him, much as she hated to admit it. It was beating terribly erratic—as wild and as primitive as the bayou at midnight.

As if sensing her gaze, Cooter looked up and caught her eye.

He checked a slow smile easing across his face. Her insides melted a little.

Marla smiled back, warmth flooding her veins.

She swallowed hard and slid onto a stool near the end. Cooter placed a Lone Star in front of her without a word.

She might avoid most men in Carrington, but she would always come back for Cooter. He was her one exception.

She took a long sip, savoring the sharp, familiar taste. "Skull Bone playing tonight?" She tried to sound casual, nonchalant, and wondered if it was working.

"Nah. Next weekend. Bayou Jam is here." Cooter's voice was a rough rumble.

"Ah." Marla took another drink of beer. "Shoot. I told Molly and Mitzi that Skull Bone was playing. I think they were going to make it up. I should text them." She pulled her phone out of her back pocket.

"You coming around again now?"

His question made her pause, and she slowly set the phone face down on the bar, the text unsent.

"I don't know." Marla traced a pattern in the condensation on her beer bottle, glancing about at the crowd, not making eye contact. "Been a few weeks."

"Eight weeks. Two months. Five days."

She met his gaze then. He knew exactly how long? "Oh."

"You're the one who left." There was an edge to Cooter's words. "Said you needed time away from this place. From me."

"I know." She held his gaze, unmoving. "But I couldn't stay away. Not from the music, and... Not from you."

Cooter stared, his expression unreadable, except for a flicker of longing in his eyes that kicked up a response of mixed messages in her heart and gut—of hope and apprehension.

She wanted him. She didn't want him. She wanted him.

The bar erupted in cheers as Bayou Jam took the stage,

launching into their first song. Marla swayed, closing her eyes and losing herself in the familiar chords and lyrics. When she opened them again, Cooter was watching her, a smile tugging at the corner of his mouth.

"Come on," he said, grabbing her hand. "Let's get out of here."

"You can't leave."

"We need to talk." Cooter glanced to his right. "Luke can handle this crowd." He gave the bartender a nod.

Marla watched Cooter's friend, Luke Strong, nod back, then slid her gaze to Cooter. Her heart nearly burst from her chest at the intense look in his eyes. "Where are we going?"

"Anywhere but here." Cooter's smile widened. "The night is young." His eyebrows waggled.

He grabbed a bottle of Jim Beam and led her out the back. Marla laughed, gripped his hand, and followed Cooter to his bike. He stashed the whiskey in a saddlebag. She climbed on behind him, her arms winding around his waist, fingers locking over his hard, taut, six-pack abdomen. The engine roared to life beneath them as they sped off.

Her chest grew warm against his back—from the inside out. She was home at last.

* * *

The night air rushed over her skin as they sped down the dark, winding roads outside of town. Marla clung to Cooter, overcome with the thrill of it all, no longer questioning her sanity.

This was right.

They arrived at the old, abandoned barn, its silhouette illuminated by the moonlight. She followed him just inside the wide door, her steps tentative but determined. He spread out a blanket on the dirt floor and opened the bottle of whiskey.

They could still see the sky. Marla noticed the clouds had cleared. Stars glittered the night sky. She relaxed a little more.

"We used to come out here a lot when we were kids." He gestured to the dusty bales of hay stacked against one wall. "My uncle owns the place."

Marla cocked her head. "Ah, hay bales, full moons, and young lovers in the night. Was this your favorite spot?"

He laughed. "No girls. Just my guy friends and me, shooting the shit, drinking some beer. Maybe sneaking a smoke." He gave her a wicked grin.

She smiled, inching closer to him until their knees touched. "I don't believe that for a minute."

He threw back his head and laughed again.

He handed her the bottle of Jim Beam. She took a sip, then handed it back. He took a gulp. The fire of the alcohol burned down her throat and filled her with warmth. Seduced by the setting, perhaps, and the man leaning in closer, Marla kissed him—slowly at first, then deeper—until she was lost in his embrace.

Cooter pulled away slightly and brushed his lips across hers again before lying back on the blanket and folding his hands beneath his head. She admired his strong features, illuminated in the moonlight, as he studied her with deep-set eyes that seemed to search through every layer of her being for answers she wasn't sure she had.

He reached for her hand, turning it over so he could trace circles around her palm with his thumb. "Tell me everything," he whispered. "Tell me the problem between us."

Marla let go of her doubts as she spoke. Her voice quavered at first, but grew stronger with emotion.

"Between us?"

He nodded. "How about you talk about how you feel about us? Period."

Marla blew out a breath. "I was feeling like what I knew about myself wasn't true anymore."

He grinned. "I get that."

"I never intended to fall for someone so completely. I don't do relationships, Cooter. I've never been good with them and, frankly, I never wanted one."

His right eyebrow spiked. "Oh? And now?"

She sighed. "I've missed you these past two months. I didn't know what we had was real until I was away from you. All I could think about was getting back to how things were before the night of the argument." She held her breath. "Do you feel the same way?"

Cooter remained silent but gripped her hand throughout her confession until finally nodding in response when she finished speaking.

"Marla, darlin', I can't get enough of you. I need you in my life." It was a simple, heartfelt statement. Just like him. Straightforward and uncomplicated.

Marla tilted her head back with a sigh and gazed up at the stars. "Oh, Cooter...."

"You're beautiful." Cooter propped himself up on an elbow.

She looked at him. "It's just the moonlight."

He touched her cheek with a forefinger, let it linger and then slowly trace the side of her face. "No, it's you."

"It's the stars." Her brain raced, trying to recall if anyone had ever called her beautiful before. Pretty, maybe, but beautiful? "The stars are beautiful."

"Not as beautiful as you." Cooter brushed a stray curl behind her ear. "I'm glad you came to Deadhead that night two years ago. You turned my universe upside down, Marla Newberry."

She looked at him, this easygoing, caring man who had

stormed into her life. "You did the same for me. I never knew I could feel this way about someone."

"Tell me how you feel?" His voice was rough with emotion.

"Like I can be fully myself with you. Like we're two parts of the same whole." She took his hand, threading their fingers together. "You're it for me, Cooter. However long we have in this life, I'm yours. If there's anything after this, I'm yours then, too."

He stared into her eyes for a long moment, as if he were measuring what to say next. Then she guessed he figured he should put it out there again.

"I love you, Marla."

She eased out a sigh and her chest felt lighter. "Cooter," she whispered, "I love you, too." She'd never said those words to another man.

Cooter pulled her in for a searing kiss. Marla gave herself over to the sensation, to him, heart, body, and soul. The next few hours sealed their love with a toe-tingling romp under the stars that Marla knew she would never forget.

They shared a bond as endless as the road ahead and as constant as the stars above. With bone-deep certainty, what they had would endure all tests of time.

Perhaps eternity.

Chapter Two

O*ne week later...*

Marla spotted her sister Molly, sitting at the bar and chatting with Brody Willis, the guy she was dating, and Luke Strong, the bartender.

Marla had actually known Brody first and had introduced him to her sister a few months ago, when they were all caught up in the drama of Molly's husband's sudden death. Private Investigator Willis had provided not only guidance and support, but backup for some of the hair-brained schemes she and her sisters had gotten into while trying to solve that murder mystery.

Which they did. Eventually. With Brody's help, of course.

Solving murders—or attempted murders—was something the sisters were collectively good at, although it was a little disturbing that each of their love interests had met with some sort of danger, demise, or death.

Mitzi's husband had gone missing, died, became a ghost

who stalked her, and then, by some magical time thing that had something to do with time travel, came back to life again. Mitzi and Ken were happily-ever-after now.

Molly's husband had died in a seven-car pileup while traveling to Alabama for a monster truck pull. While he became a ghost too, and contributed to Molly finding out who offed him, unfortunately, Don Campbell remained deceased.

Which is why Molly was now free to date the private detective.

Was Cooter in danger, too? Some sort of wicked thud landed in her gut. She glanced about. Where was her guy?

Tick. Tick. Tick.

The sound took her a little off guard—she pushed it away. *I'm ignoring you.* Nodding to Luke behind the bar, she slipped into a seat beside Molly and said, "Beer please?"

"You got it, Marla."

"Seen Cooter?"

Luke shot her a teasing grin. "Your old man's in the back. He'll be out soon."

My old man. She liked the sound of that.

"There you are." Molly turned and hugged Marla. "We were wondering if you'd show."

"And miss out on Skull Bone? Never."

"The usual, I assume." Luke sat a Lone Star in front of her.

"You know me too well," she said with a grin. Then twisting to look at Molly, asked, "Mitzi coming?"

Molly nodded. "She's on her way. Should be here soon."

"Good." Marla had been looking forward to an evening with her sisters tonight.

Marla sipped her beer, savoring the crisp, cold taste. Out of the corner of her eye, she noticed Cooter heading their way, two beers in hand.

Her pulse quickened as he approached, his smile like the

sun breaking through the clouds. She loved the way he moved, with a predatory grace that sent shivers down her spine, reminding her of the toe-tingling to come.

"Here you go, darlin'," Cooter said, handing her one of the beers. He leaned in and kissed her cheek, his scruffy beard tickling her nose.

Their fingers brushed, igniting temporary sparks. "Thanks, Cooter. Now I've got a backup."

He grinned. "The band's settin' up now. Ya'll are in for a treat tonight."

"We wouldn't miss it," Molly said.

Cooter's gaze lingered on Marla, a silent exchange passing between them. She knew if she asked, he'd take her on another adventure, just the two of them against the open road. She leaned in. "I have an idea. Let's take a road trip one of these days, maybe next summer, you and me on our bikes. We could follow the Dead bands across country and have some fun."

Cooter waggled his brows. "I like fun. Let's talk about it."

She grinned. "Groovy."

"I'll come find you after the show," he whispered, squeezing her hand. Without hesitation, he leaned in for a soft, lingering, passion-filled kiss. Pulling back only slightly, he gazed into her eyes. "I love you," he whispered.

"I love you back," she breathed. "Double."

Grinning, Cooter stepped away, smiling as if he had a secret.

Warmth flooded her cheeks. She took a hasty sip of her beer to hide her grin.

Molly elbowed her playfully. "You two are disgusting. Get a room already!"

"Oh hush," Marla said, though she couldn't contain her smile. She felt giddy-happy at the moment.

Cooter headed to the stage. Her gaze followed him like a

magnet—powerless to resist his pull, drawn to him on a level beyond reason or logic. With Cooter, she became someone new, someone free, fearless, and bold. He was her grand adventure in this life and whatever came after.

Her soul mate.

The band launched into their first song.

Marla swayed to the music, losing herself in the pounding tattoo of Cooter's drums. His rhythms were primal, visceral, tapping into something deep within her. When he looked at her from behind the drum kit, his eyes burning into hers, and she felt branded. Claimed.

Oh my. She loved that.

Later, after the set, Cooter found her at the bar. Leaning in behind her, he growled in her ear. "Wanna get out of here, woman?" Marla turned and caught his fiery gaze and sensual demeanor. He seemed a little on edge.

"What do you have in mind, lover?"

"Sex. Hot sex. And lots of it. I can't wait to strip you down to your—"

Marla stopped him with a finger to his lips. "As much as I like hot sex...." She eyed him. "You're angry. You okay?"

"Yeah." He glanced back at the stage.

"You sure?"

He didn't answer.

"Cooter? Look at me. What's wrong?"

Finally, he made eye contact. "Nothing I can't take care of, babe. Hold that hot sex thought for a minute. Just one thing I gotta do before we leave, then I'm all yours. I'll be right back." He gave her a quick hug, a lingering brush against her lips, then rushed off.

Marla watched him step back onto the stage, then turned to Molly. "Something's wrong," she whispered.

"What?"

But Marla didn't answer, her attention glued to the stage.

Cooter approach the Skull Bone's manager, Rick Landry, shouting words she couldn't hear over the din of the bar. He repeatedly poked Landry in the chest with his forefinger.

Marla half stood. The band shuffled off stage. Cooter shoved himself up against the manager in a heated argument, gesturing wildly. The manager pushed him back and Cooter went sailing into his drum kit.

A sudden silence blanketed the room.

Landry grabbed Cooter's vest, hauling him to his feet. Before Marla could get halfway across the bar, Cooter cocked the guy square in the jaw and sent him sailing into wings off stage. Cooter followed, vanishing behind a cloud of smoke.

Molly joined Marla. "Did you see that?"

"Yeah. What the f— I'm going to go see what's going on."

"I saw it." Luke stepped up and grasped Marla's arm, holding her back. "Let him go. Give him a minute. He's not in a mood to talk, I'm sure. He'll be back."

"Do you know what that was about?" She searched Luke's face.

"Maybe. Kind of."

"Tell me."

"I can't, Marla. Cooter said to keep it hush."

She opened her mouth to say something smart-ass but stopped short at the sight of Brody shouldering through the crowd. She hadn't realized he'd left the bar. Marla's heart thudded as he made a beeline for them.

Brody's expression was grim. "Where's Cooter heading off to?"

Marla squared herself in front of him. "What do you mean?"

"He just sped out of here on his bike like a house afire. He was leaving as I was coming back in from a smoke."

Luke pushed closer. "Anyone else leaving?"

"Looked like he was following another bike."

"Landry?" Luke turned away, pacing. "The band's manager. Shit."

Marla's stomach lurched, and she staggered a little. Molly steadied her with a gentle hand on her arm. "I'm sure there's a reasonable explanation."

But Marla knew better. The memory of Cooter's anger flickered behind her eyes, and a chill ran down her spine. She glanced at the shadows clinging to the stage, feeling the weight of unseen eyes on her skin. Something was wrong.

* * *

Marla's stomach churned as she listened to the gossip swirl around her. They gathered at the bar now—Luke, Brody, and Marla—mulling over what had happened and things they'd heard. Molly had drifted off to somewhere. According to some bar patrons up front, a rival drummer made a deal with the Skull Bone manager. A deal that Cooter apparently didn't like.

He was upset—but what was he up to, speeding off like that? Was he in trouble? Going after the guy? Taking a deep breath, she grasped Luke's arm. "Is that true? What was the deal? What do you know?"

Luke took a breath. "He'd heard the rumors—Cooter, that is. Guess it all came to a head tonight. Appears this was Cooter's last Skull Bone show. Landry contracted with a new drummer."

"Why?" This made no sense.

"I'm not sure, Marla. We will find out when Cooter gets back."

If he comes back. The notion sent chills down her spine.

"We have to find him." She looked at Brody. She wasn't

above begging. "Please. That's what you do, right? Find people?"

Brody studied her for a long moment before giving a curt nod. "Yeah. Sometimes. Look, I'll get on it...but until I figure out what's going on, you—and your sisters—lie low. Got it?"

She nodded. "Sure."

He stared. "I mean it. Do not go off on your Harley looking for him. I don't need two missing people to search for."

Marla gritted her teeth. She didn't need protecting, but she swallowed her protests and forced a tight smile. "Got it."

His urgent words worried her, though. Did he know more than what he was telling her?

Brody melted into the crowd, leaving Marla with a gnawing sense that this was only the beginning of something bad.

Glancing at Luke, she said, "Bourbon. Straight. Now."

He quickly obliged.

Molly strode back from across the room and sank onto a bar stool. "Hey. What's going on? I was in the restroom."

Marla clutched her tumbler. "Not sure." The amber liquid sloshed over the rim, dripping onto the bar. Her fingers trembled, and she took a deep breath to steady herself. Without looking at her sister, she asked, "Mitzi here yet?"

"No." Molly shook her head. "She texted. She and Ken are doing date night since he was out of town last weekend."

"Oh."

Molly edged closer. Silence fell between them, broken only by the raucous laughter of the surrounding bar patrons.

"I heard some talking," Molly offered. "They say that guy hanging with the manager—the one with the scraggly beard?— made some kind of deal for the drummer job." She dropped her voice to a whisper. "Word is, Cooter is out."

"We heard that." Marla's grip tightened around the glass. "Brody's looking into it. But Cooter just wouldn't leave like that... Not without saying goodbye." She swallowed hard against the lump forming in her throat. "We had plans. Something's wrong. I can feel it."

Molly sighed, wrapping an arm around Marla's shoulders. "I know, sweetie. But Brody's on it. He'll sort this out." Her smile didn't quite reach her eyes. "Cooter's a tough son of a gun. I'm sure he's fine."

Marla forced a nod, though her doubts remained. She stared into her glass again, watching the light dance across the amber liquid. The gnawing sense of dread only grew deeper, and a single thought repeated in her mind like a mantra:

Where are you, Cooter? And what have you gotten yourself into?

Tick. Tick. Tick.

Shut up!

Hours passed, the bar crowd thinned, and there was still no word from Cooter. Marla paced the length of the bar, clutching her phone so tightly her knuckles turned white. She kept calling his number, only to reach his voicemail every time.

Finally, Luke pulled her aside, grasping her shoulders firmly. "Hey. You need to calm down. I'm sure there's an explanation for all this." His blue eyes were soft with concern. "You look dead on your feet. Go home and get some rest."

Marla shook her head, panic rising in her chest. "I can't. Not until I know he's okay."

"How about you go upstairs to Cooter's apartment and take a nap then?"

She eyed him for a second. "No, Luke."

A heavy sigh escaped his lips as he ran a hand through his hair. "I understand, but it won't do Cooter any good if you make yourself sick with worry. I'll keep calling around and let you know the second I hear anything."

The pleading look in his eyes crumbled her resolve. She

nodded slowly, exhaustion seeping into her bones. "You're right. I'm no use to anyone like this. I'll go upstairs."

Luke's answering smile was strained but warm. "That's my girl. Now go get some sleep." He gave her hands a gentle squeeze before releasing them. "I'll be here if you need me."

Marla bid her sister goodbye with a hug, then headed for the back room and the stairwell to the second-level apartment. But before she took even five steps, Brody burst through the entrance, eyes wild, frantically looking about.

"Marla, wait," he gasped, clutching at her arm. "There's been an accident."

Her heart leaped into her throat. "What?"

"I'm so sorry."

Molly raced to her sister. "Oh, shit."

Marla grabbed Brody's shirt, balling the fabric up in her fists, panic surging through her veins. "Cooter. Is he...?" She couldn't bring herself to say the word. *Dead?*

Brody's face crumpled in a mask of sorrow. "His bike rolled and slid into a gulley off the highway, heading toward Killeen. He's missing, and there is a search team, but he's presumed..."

Dead.

At that moment, Marla's world came crashing down around her.

Chapter Three

The sofa in her living room became her world. Marla lay curled up in the darkened room, clutching Cooter's faded leather jacket. The weather outside was humid and sunny, but the mood inside her small apartment was the exact opposite. She'd turned down the air conditioning; the room was icy cold, with rivulets of condensation forming on the windows. Breathing in the familiar scent of motor oil and pine, fresh tears welled in her eyes.

Her heart ached like the throb of an infected wound; she couldn't summon the strength to face her students. While being a little social might be beneficial for her, she knew there was no such thing as "a little bit social" when you teach middle school. She called in sick for the week.

It was Monday morning, approximately thirty-two hours since Cooter vanished into the night, his motorcycle skidding off the road into that ravine. They had dragged the river but only found his cracked and dented helmet downstream from where his bike landed. According to the police, the investigation was ongoing. The news of the accident was all over the television and social media.

Luke and Brody and a couple of guys in Cooter's motor-cycle club traveled to the accident spot to retrieve the bike. She'd heard from Luke that they were going to restore it and put it in the bar at Deadhead, in honor of Cooter.

Marla shook her head, trying to clear the images from her mind. *He's not dead!* She wanted to scream at him. *Just wait!* But all she could do was fade into the worn leather, an attempt to escape this waking nightmare.

Just as she'd settled into a pleasant state of drowsy, the front door of her apartment burst open. Molly and Mitzi rushed in, arms laden with grocery bags. "We're not taking no for an answer," Mitzi said, her voice brooking no argument. "We have food."

Marla groaned. "Thanks, but I told you both I want to be left alone."

"You need to get off this sofa," Molly urged, throwing open the curtains and flooding the room with light.

"Ow. That hurts." Marla pulled the covers over her head.

Molly tugged the blanket. "Come on, sis. Let us help you."

"Leave me alone," Marla mumbled.

But Molly was persistent, yanking the blankets away and forcing her to confront the world outside her self-imposed cocoon.

"You have to eat," Mitzi said.

Molly sat on the edge of the couch. "You can't keep hiding from life. Cooter wouldn't want that."

"Easy for you to say," Marla snapped, jerking the comforter away from her face, tears welling up in her eyes. "You didn't lose him."

"Maybe not," Molly admitted, "but we know loss. And we're worried about you. We just want our sister back. When are you going to face the fact that Cooter's gone?"

Marla sat up with a scowl. "Don't say that! He's not gone,

he's missing, that's all." Deep down, she knew the truth. But she couldn't give up hope. Not yet. "In fact, we should look harder for him. I should be looking."

"You need rest." Mitzi stepped closer. "Your body has been through an emotional shock and it's still fresh. Come on, we have potato salad, pimento cheese, watermelon, and chocolate éclair ice cream."

"From the Dairy Barn?"

"You betcha. Let's eat."

Marla sighed, knowing her sisters were right, although she was reluctant to admit it even to herself. She missed Cooter more than anything—and she'd wasted the past two months, let time slip away—but if she let her grief swallow her whole, she'd never find a way to live without him.

How could this have happened? She'd finally given herself over to love, only to have it yanked away from her. And why in the world would Cooter risk that? Why did he go off all half-cocked and loaded for bear on his bike?

Had something more transpired between him and the band manager than the drummer gig?

I'll likely never know.

"Fine," she halfheartedly conceded, pulling herself into a sitting position. "I'll try."

"Good," Molly smiled, relief washing over her face. "Now let's get some lunch, then maybe we can run to the mall or something. See a movie? Take your mind off things. Get dressed."

"And shower first," Mitzi added. "You kinda stink."

Marla stood, the comforter falling, and rolled her eyes. "Fine!"

* * *

"Marla," Molly gripped her sister's hand. "I know this is hard, but you can't let Cooter's death consume you like this. Find a way to move forward."

They'd lunched, and Marla had showered and dressed, and then they'd ended up in the mall seeing the latest Tom Cruise action-adventure movie—which Marla had mostly slept through —and now sat at a table in the middle of the busy food court, eating loaded fries and drinking sodas.

Marla scoffed. "How am I supposed to do that when I don't know what happened to him?"

Her phone buzzed on the table. She grabbed it up when she saw the name on the screen: Brody Willis. "Hello?"

She eyed her sisters.

"Marla, we need to talk," Brody said in a grim tone. "Got a minute?"

What in the world? "Yes. What's going on?"

Molly leaned closer.

"Things aren't adding up with Cooter's accident."

Marla gasped. "Why?"

"I'm talking foul play."

"Good Lord, Brody. What the hell?"

"Can we meet?"

"Yes!" She had to know the truth, no matter how much it hurt. For Cooter's sake, she had to find out what really happened that night. She steeled herself. "We're at the mall food court. Where are you?"

"Ten minutes away. See you soon." He clicked off.

Marla stared at her sisters and let go of a shallow breath. "Brody's on his way here. He thinks there was foul play."

"Shit." Mitzi stood. "I need a refill."

"I need a beer."

"I wish," Molly echoed.

For the next several minutes, they sipped their soft drinks and chatted, waiting for Brody.

"Who would want to hurt Cooter? That doesn't make sense," Molly said.

"Everyone liked him," Mitzi added.

"I loved him." Marla mumbled the words, then slowly lifted her gaze to look her sisters in the eyes. "I did. I don't get it."

"Maybe I can help with that."

The sisters jumped.

Turning, Marla caught Brody's eye, his expression somber.

"I want to know everything, Brody. Everything."

He nodded. "All right."

"Hold nothing back. I mean it. Sit." She motioned to the chair beside Molly.

He flashed Molly a quick grin. She smiled back. "I've been looking into what happened. I'm thinking it wasn't an accident at all."

"Wait, what?" Marla's heart skipped a beat, her grief momentarily replaced by shock. "What do you mean?"

Brody glanced about, as if someone might be listening. "I don't have all the pieces yet, but something's not right."

"You have his bike, right?"

Brody nodded. "Yes, and I went all over the scene. That's what led me to doing some deeper investigation. Someone could have tampered with his bike. Or, he could have been forced off the road."

"But the police in Texas said it looked like his bike skid on the oily road."

"I'm not buying that."

"Who would want to kill Cooter?" Marla's voice shook. Suddenly, she felt both fearful and angry.

"Can't say for sure yet," Brody admitted. He ran a hand

through his unkempt hair. "But I think we need to investigate further, and I could use your help."

"Us?" Molly raised an eyebrow. "What could we possibly do?"

"Y'all were close to Cooter, knew him better than anyone," Brody countered, meeting Marla's eyes. "If anyone can help me figure out who'd want to hurt him, it's you."

Marla hesitated, torn between her desire for answers and the fear that delving into Cooter's accident would only plunge her deeper into darkness—or unveil something she'd be better off not knowing. "I don't know. Maybe we should leave it alone."

Mitzi sat straight up. "Marla! You don't want to do that."

Molly reached for her hand on the table. "Honey, you're gonna want to know the truth."

Brody interjected. "Well, with your help or not, I'm not letting things go. Cooter was my friend. And I have to wonder if someone was out to murder him. And if so, does that put any of the rest of us in danger?"

Icy trepidation skipped down Marla's spine. "Brody, you're being ridiculous," she snapped. "Cooter may have had a few enemies, but no one would actually want to kill him."

Brody's gaze penetrated. "Marla, I know it's hard to accept, but we need to face the possibility that someone wanted Cooter dead."

She shook her head, unwilling to believe that anyone could harbor such hatred for the man she loved. As much as she craved answers, Marla couldn't bear the thought of digging deeper into the circumstances of Cooter's death. She needed to grieve, to heal, not throw herself headlong into danger.

"Brody, is it possible this was just a horrible accident? Nothing else?"

He peered straight into her eyes. "Want my professional opinion, given what I know about the crime scene?"

She nodded.

"No. I do not believe this was an accident. Someone wanted him dead."

His words cut to her core. Shouldering up, she braced herself. "Thanks, Brody, but we'll pass," Marla said firmly, standing and turning away from them all. "Let's go, girls."

She didn't look back or wait to see if they followed her out of the food court.

* * *

That night, Marla tossed and turned in her bed, her mind plagued with thoughts of Cooter—his laugh, his touch, the way his eyes lit up when he saw her. The last sexy words he growled to her right before all hell broke loose.

Brody's words echoed in her mind, too. Who would want to hurt Cooter? He was the kindest, most caring man she'd ever known. Oh, he was gruff and tough on the outside, but on the inside, at least with her, he was tender and loving. The thought of someone deliberately causing him harm made her blood boil.

Sleep finally claimed her, but it was restless and fitful.

And apparently, only for a few minutes. She woke with a start, disoriented by the sudden transition from dream to reality. Blinking against the darkness, moonlight streaming through her window, she listened for something she wasn't sure she had heard.

Silence.

A visual sensation of a man manifested at the foot of her bed. She gasped.

"Hello, darlin'."

"Cooter?" Her heart beat a wild cadence against her chest wall.

Is this a dream, or really happening?

The vision faced in and out, like a hologram or a ghostly image. Marla rubbed her eyes in disbelief. It was Cooter, dressed in his usual faded jeans and leather vest, with his scruffy beard and longish hair, a confused expression on his pale, translucent face.

"What is happening?"

The vision spoke again. "To tell you the truth, I'm not sure."

"Are you a ghost?"

Cooter gazed, a solemn expression on his face. "I'm so sorry, darlin'. I never meant to leave you like that, stranded in the bar. I meant to come right back."

Marla trembled. How could this be happening? Yet one look into Cooter's eyes and she knew, without a doubt, that it was him. Her Cooter. And he was in trouble.

Reaching out a shaking hand, she wanted nothing more than to touch him again, but her hand passed right through his misty form.

"Marla, darlin'," the ghostly figure whispered, his voice a mere echo of his former self. "If I'm dead, I'm extremely disappointed. I expected to see Patsy Cline, some of the Skynyrd band, or Jerry Garcia by now. If there's no southern rock in Heaven, then I'd just as soon...."

"Cooter. Don't say that!"

Her breath caught in her throat, a mixture of fear and sorrow washing over her. The image of Cooter was translucent, barely more than an ethereal wisp of the man she'd known, but she couldn't deny the connection she felt to him in that moment.

"You're not...gone. I refuse to believe it." She couldn't bring herself to say *dead*.

"I need your help, baby."

"How?" Her voice was barely a whisper.

"I'm not sure where I am. I'm...stuck, I think."

"What?"

"Someone... Someone tried killed me," his spirit murmured, his eyes filled with sadness. "I can't rest until I know who did it. But I also need your help right now, before I totally fade away."

She sat up on her knees. "Oh my God, Cooter. Where are you?"

"I don't know. It's dark. Wet. I feel...suspended."

"Are you...alive?"

Marla's heart clenched with pain, but this time, she couldn't dismiss the possibility so easily. That Cooter's restless spirit sat before her was proof enough that something wasn't right.

"I don't think so. I feel...in between. Help me."

"Of course," she whispered, tears streaming down her cheeks. "I'll help you, Cooter. I promise."

A faint smile lit Cooter's face. "I knew I could count on you, darlin'. You are the strongest, most stubborn woman I ever met. I just wish this was all some bad dream...." His voice trailed off as he faded into the night, leaving Marla alone once more.

"Maybe it is," she whispered. "A terrible dream."

She clutched her blankets tight, fresh tears sliding down her cheeks. Cooter needed her help. Whatever this was, it was a message. A cry for help.

And somehow, she wasn't going to let him down.

Chapter Four

Marla: *9-1-1 ladies. My place. Stat!*
Mitzi: *It's middle of da night.*
Marla: *Wake Molly up.*
Mitzi: God, Marla.
Molly: *WTF?*
Marla: *ASAP.*
Molly: *Kids*
Marla: *What?*
Molly: *Can't leave kids.*
Marla: *Geez. Morning then? Drop kids at Mom's. I need you.*
Mitzi: *Shit. What is it?*

Marla paused for a moment before responding. Should she just dump it on them in text, or wait?

Mitzi: *Marla?*
Marla: *Get here by 8. I have coffee.*

* * *

Her sisters arrived early, concern etched on their sleep-swollen faces. Marla took a deep breath, ready for the onslaught. "Coffee's in the kitchen," she said, turning away from the door.

"We brought donuts."

"Awesome." Marla glanced back. "We may need them." Donuts had sustained them on many a ghost-hunting, murder-solving adventure.

"I bought two dozen." Molly set the flat box of donuts on the counter. "Okay, sister. What gives? You sounded desperate last night."

"Not desperate." Marla opened the box and perused the contents. Good gracious. Glazed. Cream horns. Chocolate cake with sprinkles. A half-dozen donut holes. She chose a raspberry Bismark. "Have to tell you something."

"Second thoughts about helping Brody?" Mitzi picked up a donut hole, popped it in her mouth, then made a beeline for the coffeemaker. "Thank God. This blend smells heavenly. What is it?"

"I just added a cinnamon stick." Marla took her coffee and jelly donut to the living room and set both on the coffee table. "Get over here and listen carefully." She maintained a firm voice, despite her exhaustion. "Cooter came to me last night. He needs my help. Our help."

"Excuse me?" Mitzi sat across from her in the recliner, her right brow arched.

"He came to me. His ghost, I mean. I think."

Molly halted and stared. "You think? You think what?"

She cleared her throat. "I mean, I think he was a ghost. It was weird. I was awake but I could have been dreaming. Either way, Cooter sent a message." She met Molly's gaze. "You have experience in this department. What did Don look like when he was a ghost?"

Shrugging, Molly sat in the rocker. "Sort of see-through.

Sometimes he was more body-like than others. The closer I got to solving the murder, the more I could see him and then suddenly, poof, he was gone forever."

"Hm." She looked at Mitzi. "What about Ken?"

"Same. He floated a lot. He was his full-bodied self but transparent and sort of glowy." She thought for a second. "Except when we put him in the freezer with the blackberries."

"Right." That was a day she'd just as soon forget. Sighing, she took a drink of coffee. "Cooter wasn't any of those things. He was kind of misty and cloudy, more of a vision than a ghost."

"Maybe he's not fully dead." Molly shrugged.

Marla and Mitzi stared.

Molly's eyes went wide. "Well, you know, Ken was freshly dead when Mitzi found him. And Don was like...seriously dead after that truck crash. No doubting he was a goner. We couldn't even have an open casket, remember? Maybe Cooter isn't fully dead yet?"

"Sometimes..." Marla muttered. "Your brain...."

Molly scooted closer. "They haven't found his body yet, right? Maybe he's still alive somewhere, but unconscious."

Mitzi chucked her shoulder. "Stop. Don't get her hopes up, girl!"

"Or," Molly went on. "He could be gratefully dead. You know. Like the band. Since he plays in a Dead cover band and all. And maybe he's grateful since a motorcycle accident had to be painful...and what if a coyote dragged him off?"

Mitzi stood abruptly. "Molly, shut up! Where's your compassion? My God!"

Molly's face froze. "Well. Sorry."

"Wait." Marla stood, ignoring them. She couldn't be bothered with Molly's ditziness now. She'd learned to ignore that years ago. Besides, something about what Molly said niggled. Pacing in the living room, she took a moment, then turned back.

"Maybe you're right. He said he felt in between, and he didn't know if he was dead or not. If you were a ghost, you'd know you were dead. Right?"

The sisters nodded.

"He said he needs our help. That someone tried to kill him."

"So Brody was right."

"Yes. Maybe he can't get unstuck until we find his attempted killer."

"Or maybe he's lying out there in pain somewhere, needing medical attention," Molly added.

Mitzi shot her a look.

"Well, it happens!" Molly argued.

Marla put herself between them. "Or, maybe he's not out there in the Texas hillside at all. Maybe someone kidnapped him. Maybe... Maybe he was having an out-of-body experience and floated into my dream."

Molly blinked several times. "You could be on to something."

"No," Mitzi interrupted. "I don't think it works like that. The almost dead person is the one who has the out-of-body experience. They don't float into other people's unconsciousness."

"Or consciousness?" A bit frustrated, Marla turned away from her sisters, thinking. What all this meant, she didn't know. They were operating on speculation here and couldn't do a damn thing about it until they found some hard evidence.

"But who would kidnap him?"

Marla turned to Mitzi. "God only knows." She rubbed her temples. "But we have to find out. For Cooter's sake. You'll help, right?"

"Count me in," Molly said immediately, her impulsive nature shining through. "We'll get justice for Cooter, no matter what."

"Of course, we'll help," Mitzi agreed, her calm demeanor a source of stability. "But we have to be careful. If that's the case, then whoever did this is dangerous."

"And we should tell Brody."

"Yes, we should. Thank you both. I couldn't do it without the two of you."

"Hey, we're sisters," Molly chimed in with a grin. "This is what we do—stick together and kick some serious butt."

"Let's just focus on finding out who was after Cooter first, and why," Mitzi interjected, a hint of humor in her voice as she tempered Molly's enthusiasm. "Then we can decide on the appropriate amount of butt-kicking."

The weight of her worries lifted. Marla's eyes welled with tears as she looked between her sisters. "Thank you. I knew I could count on you two. Question is, where do we start?"

"At the beginning," Mitzi said. "We need to retrace Cooter's last steps. See who might have had it out for him. Find out if anyone overheard the conversation between Cooter and that band manager."

"That means we need to go to Deadhead. Is it still open?"

"I heard Luke is opening up tonight," Mitzi responded.

"Good."

"We need to call Brody. Have him meet us there."

Marla smiled. "Yes, Molly. We'll call your new BF Brody. I'm sure we can use his help." She knocked back the last of her coffee. "Let's do this."

"On it." Mitzi stood, taking her cup into the kitchen.

"Behind you." Molly followed.

Marla grinned. The Newberry sisters were on the hunt once more.

* * *

Late afternoon, Marla slipped into Deadhead, glancing around the semi-crowded and smoky establishment looking for her sisters. Spying Molly sitting alone at a tall table near the bar, she shouldered through a few guys playing pool to reach her.

"Hey." She shrugged out of her jacket and draped it over the back of a chair. "Mitzi coming?"

Molly nodded. "On her way. I have bad news though."

"What?" Bad news was not what she wanted to hear.

"Brody had to go out of town. Arson investigation down in New Orleans. Some fire on Bourbon Street. You know he's a certified arson investigator."

"No, I didn't know that."

"He is."

"Well, shit."

"Yeah. I know. He said to tell you he's sorry and for us to call him if we get any news or info."

Marla rubbed her temple. A nagging pain had settled there since last night. "Let's talk it through once Mitzi gets here."

"Sure thing." Molly stared off behind her. "Incoming directly behind you. Be careful."

Turning, she found herself face to face with the Skull Bone's manager—Rick Landry, she thought that was his name. Her last memory of him was Cooter poking him in the chest with his forefinger, then watching him sail backward off the stage.

The guy's beady eyes narrowed as he approached. "Well, if it ain't the grieving girlfriend." He let out a nasty chuckle.

Marla stiffened, refusing to cower. Internally, she cringed, and her stomach pitched. "Funny seeing you here. I have some questions about Saturday night."

"I know nothin' about that other than the asshole went off half-cocked on me. Crazy son-of-a-bitch." He sneered. "Now get outta my bar before I have to throw you out."

"Your bar? I don't think so. It's Cooter's."

"Mine now, sweetheart. I can even show you the papers."

What the hell is he talking about?

"We'll see about that. No way Cooter would give his bar to you."

The guy chuckled and crowded closer. "Giving had nothing to do with it, sweetheart. It's only a matter of time and technicality."

He moved in closer, but Marla wasn't backing down. If he thought he intimidated her, he had another thing coming. She taught middle-schoolers. "Well. I'll chat with my lawyer about that. The police, too."

"You do that, missy. Won't change a damn thing. Now why don't you get out of here while you can?"

While I can?

"Unless you'd like to join me in a bit of afternoon delight?"

"Oh, that's gross," Molly bit out.

Anger rose in Marla's chest, hot and bitter. She wanted to slap him and contemplated doing that for about half a second until a firm hand grasped her arm.

"That's enough." Luke Strong's gravelly tone broke into the argument. "Marla has every right to be here, Landry, and you're out of line."

"Way out of line," Molly echoed, standing beside Luke now.

The man grunted and chuckled.

Luke glared at Landry, his gaze unwavering.

Finally, he stepped back. "I'm going. But you two better watch yourselves. I'll be back when the place is mine." He peered into Marla's eyes, then shifted to stare at Luke. "You might as well look for a job, handsome, because as soon as the new deed is inked, you're out of here."

Luke snorted and stepped closer to the guy. "Not happening."

Landry broke their stare and sauntered away.

"That's a nasty human," Marla said.

"Slimy and creepy," Molly added.

"And you two need to stay out of his way." Luke let go of Marla's elbow.

"Thank you." A wave of relief washed over her. "I may have hit him if you hadn't intervened."

"Don't thank me yet," Luke replied, his tone grim. He gestured for the women to sit at a high-top table.

Bending forward, his voice low, he said, "Look. Landry hangs with a gang that is bad news, a dangerous bunch. They are all over the Shreveport music scene. If they think you're digging into their business, they won't hesitate to put a hurt on you...or get rid of you."

Marla's stomach twisted as Luke continued.

"I suggest you leave this one alone. Let Brody handle it. He'll be back soon. It doesn't sound like something you want to take on without some backup."

"I'm not giving up on Cooter," Marla told him. "He needs me."

Luke eyed her, a questioning look on his face.

Molly shifted beside her sister. "We can handle it."

Suddenly, Mitzi swept up to the table and sat with a plop. "And you know whatever they are in for, I'm with them." She glanced about. "Hey. Sorry. I'm late."

Luke raised an eyebrow before releasing a lengthy breath and leaning back in his chair. "Alright then." A faint smile played across his lips.

Leaning into the group, Molly said, "We could sure use your help, Luke. Brody was called off to New Orleans."

"Oh?" Mitzi glanced from sister to sister.

Luke nodded. "I know. He stopped by this morning and left a box of things he'd gathered yesterday. You know I'd do anything for Cooter. And I consider all three of you good friends."

Marla sighed, watching his face. He'd been Cooter's ally for a long time. Reaching out, she found his hand on the table and covered it. "Thank you."

His gaze tangled with hers. "I'm all for closing this place down right now and us getting to work. How about it?"

"I'm game."

"Let's do it."

"On it."

Chapter Five

"The answer is here somewhere," Marla said out loud. Several hours had passed, and her head was throbbing. "Maybe we just need to look at this from a new angle."

Rubbing her gritty eyes, she gazed out over the clutter of papers strewn across the bar. Empty Lone Star bottles and a platter of half-eaten nachos occupied the spaces where there were no papers.

They'd spent the afternoon and evening immersed in the investigation—her sisters, Luke, and herself—combing through Brody's box of police reports, crime scene photos, and some interview notes. Apparently, Brody had discussed the incident with a few people who had crossed paths with Cooter in the days leading up to the accident.

His notes showed a couple of witnesses reported seeing a mysterious stranger lurking around the bar shortly before Skull Bone took the stage that night. Several mentioned the mystery person, but no one recognized him or could provide a decent description. One person thought he had a short beard. Brody also had a flyer which listed all the clubs and bars that Skull Bone had played in the past month.

It all seemed rather random.

Nothing quite added up.

Each new clue only deepened the mystery. Footage from the bar's security cameras had been deleted—Luke speculated it could have been Landry, but they knew nothing for certain. Cooter's laptop had provided a few leads. Cooter always kept it in the safe, which Luke had access to. The laptop was not password protected. He hated passwords. His bank account log-in was saved in the device, too, so they accessed his bank and other bar records.

Marla felt a little weird going through his personal stuff, but Luke convinced her they needed to explore everything. Turned out he was right. Cooter's financial records showed some interesting facts. They even found cash receipts in the safe, where Cooter had paid on a loan from Landry monthly and on time.

Why was Cooter paying him? Did it have to do with the bar?

"Make no sense," Luke said. "The bar was making money and Cooter never indicated a problem with finances."

"His checking account has plenty of funds," Marla added. "I haven't a clue."

Molly and Mitzi had conked out on them hours ago—Molly slept curled up on the sofa in Cooter's office, and Mitzi had made a temporary cot out of a couple of bar tables. Marla let them rest. They could take over for her when she was too tired to hold her head up—which could be soon.

Frustration gnawed with each dead end, but with Luke's steady presence, she persisted. His quiet confidence kept her going. "I've looked at this from every angle imaginable. Nothing makes sense."

"Then stop trying to make sense of it," Luke said. "Clear

your mind and trust your instincts. Let the evidence speak for itself."

She closed her eyes, took a deep breath, and allowed her thoughts to empty. In the silence, a faint tingle of awareness crept over her. Some minor detail teased at the edge of her awareness, as if her subconscious had pieced together a clue her cognizant mind had missed.

Her eyes flew open as the answer struck her with sudden clarity. "The deposits," she breathed. "Once a month and for a thousand dollars each time. How many were there?"

"Four, I think." Luke stared off. "Those were direct deposits, too, not cash. Cooter dealt mostly in cash. Either he or I went to the bank on Thursdays and made the cash deposits. The payments from credit cards came in on the first of the month. I don't know of any other income streams he had—but honestly, we didn't talk about stuff like that much. Did you?"

Marla had to admit she didn't know much about Cooter's personal dealings. How well did she really know him, other than he was good in the sack? "No. I don't know...."

Luke studied her. "He was a good guy, Marla. Don't second guess yourself."

Her gaze lifted and met his. "I know. I'm just suddenly realizing all I didn't know about him, and what else is out there?"

Luke touched her hand. "Now's not the time."

She nodded, shaking off her melancholy. "So, what about those deposits? I keep thinking about what Landry said—that the bar would be his in a matter of time and technicality. What did he mean?"

"I don't know." Luke's eyes lit up. "Maybe Cooter was taking a payoff to keep quiet about something? That's why they had to silence him—to stop making payments."

"You mean like blackmail? Hush money?" Marla felt a dagger-like pain in her chest. "But why?"

"I haven't a clue."

Yawning, she covered her mouth with the back of her hand. "I think it's tied to The Deadhead. If Cooter were out of the picture, then the payments would stop. Whatever secret Cooter was keeping would die with him, and perhaps even the bar was up for grabs. I swear, this has Landry's name written all over it. Do you think?"

Luke stood and put his hands on her shoulders. "I think it's a theory worth investigating. We have no proof of anything."

"So we need to get to work." Yawning again, she thumbed through another stack of papers.

"No. Get some sleep. We can do this later. Go upstairs and get in Cooter's bed. I'll wake you in a couple of hours. I'm going to catch a few winks myself, then we'll plan for the next steps."

She wanted to protest, but she didn't. Quietly leaving Luke, she headed toward the back stairs, Cooter's apartment, and his bed. She didn't even try to blink away the tears when they came.

* * *

"Damn it," Marla muttered later with a sigh. "We're going to find out who did this to you. I swear it."

Fluffing Cooter's pillows, she lay between his sheets and inhaled the scent of her man. That calmed her somewhat. She imagined his big arms wrapped around her, holding her close, the warmth of his breath tickling her ear.

Her head swam with clues and details about events leading up to the accident, but the fact remained, they did not know what happened to Cooter on that lonely highway to Killeen—and right now, she didn't want to think about the accident. She only wanted to think about how she'd loved being in the arms of the man she loved.

"Oh, Cooter. I miss you. I wish you were here."

Her eyes fluttered close, and her mind drifted. An image of Cooter on his bike, driving hell-bent-for-leather into the night, came into her head. Then suddenly, another bike came careening up behind him, edging him toward the shoulder.

Cooter swerved and righted the bike again, looking back.

The other bike sped up, heading toward him.

Cooter sped off again.

Suddenly, a large vehicle—a truck?—popped over the hill ahead, headlights illuminating the scene. She could see the silhouettes of the two bikes. The one to the right flew off out of sight. The other bike careened left. The truck split the space between them.

Then nothing. Her mind, and the scene, went black.

Marla spiked up in the bed, gasping. "Cooter!" Grappling for the bedside lamp, she turned it on. Light flooded the room. She glanced at the beside clock—had she really slept for over an hour?

Seemed like seconds.

"I'm sorry you had to see that, darlin'."

Blinking, she squinted and rubbed her eyes. Cooter sat at the foot of her bed. A vision of him, anyway.

"What just happened?" Her words rushed out on a breath.

"What did you see, babe?"

She breathed a sigh. "You, on your bike. Then another one. And a truck... Oh, God."

The bed shifted a little, as if Cooter's ethereal body had moved closer. The bed sheets wrinkled and made an indentation. "I really didn't want you to see that, but you probably should."

"Someone ran you off the road?"

"I think the truck was coincidence. The other bike, though, not so much. Plus, my brakes suddenly didn't work."

Marla leaned forward. "How are you talking to me?" She

understood ghosts—her sisters had had close encounters with the ghosts of their husbands—but was this the same thing?

The vision wavered in and out. "I'm fading, darlin'. Pretty sure my time is short. I'm leaning closer to Southern Rock Band Heaven than being here with you. I think, anyway."

"Wait." She grasped the sheets, bunching them up in her fists. "Cooter, I don't understand. Are you dead or alive? Are you injured and hurt, lying somewhere waiting for someone to find you?" It was a theory they'd tossed about and right now, suddenly, she needed to know. "Do I have hope you will come back to me?"

Her hands suddenly felt warm, like he had taken her hands in his. "Sweetheart, I'm gone—gratefully. I lingered for a while, but now fear I am crossing over."

Gratefully dead.

"How do you know?"

"I know. My days, maybe hours, are few. I can't waste them."

Marla shifted closer to his voice. "Cooter, tell me. Who did this to you? Who is responsible? Who was on that other bike?"

A warmth, like a breath, wafted over her face, drifted down her chest and body. Cooter remained silent for several ticks of her heart, then he said, "I love you, darlin'. Have for a long time. I'll be your angel—your guardian. Don't try to avenge my death. It is what it is, sweetheart."

"Oh, Cooter. I love you too. I'm such an ass. I wasted so much time."

Her face warmed, as if he had encased her cheeks in his big hands. "My sweet. No worries. I'm always in your heart...."

"Oh, Cooter."

Suddenly, it was like he'd take a step back. In a quiet voice, he added, "Don't trust Landry."

"What does he want, Cooter?"

"Don't let him get the bar."

The vision, again, faded in and out. Her cheeks, her hands went cool again. "Cooter!" From somewhere far away, she heard him say, "Sorry...."

"Cooter!" she screamed again.

But he was gone. No vision. No shifting bed. No crumpled sheets.

Right then, Luke flew into the room, looking confused and concerned. "Marla? You okay?"

She nodded. "I... I think so."

"Dream?"

Shaking her head, she contemplated what to say to Luke. "No. I mean, yes. Sort of."

He hesitantly stepped closer. "Need company?"

Honestly, she didn't. "No. I just want to go back to sleep." *I need to process this alone.*

"I get that."

"Thanks, Luke."

He moved closer to the door. "I'm just downstairs if you need anything."

Again, she nodded. "Thanks, Luke." *You're a good guy.* "I'm fine."

"Good."

* * *

The next day, after everyone had gotten some rest and a decent meal, Marla and the girls mapped out a plan.

The three headed into Shreveport. Their goal? Infiltrate the seedy underbelly of Shreveport's music scene and gather intel. They'd start with the bars and casino clubs where Cooter had recently played, according to the flyer in Brody's things, searching for leads. The area was casually known as music row, because of the music joints lining the street heading toward the river. They'd already given themselves the pep talk about watching their drinks, always answering phones and texts, and not leaving with anyone whose last name wasn't Newberry.

"Luke is going to crap when he learns we came without him," Mitzi said.

"Forget Luke! It's Brody I'm worried about." Molly glanced behind her. "I love music and a good bar hop, sisters, but I have to admit I've never been to this side of town."

"It's been at least a decade for me," Marla admitted.

"Two weeks for me," Mitzi said.

Her sisters stared.

"What? Ken likes music," she explained.

"Whatever." Molly rolled her eyes.

"Alright, ladies. Let's split up."

While she wasn't worried about Luke—who had his own agenda at Cooter's bar later tonight—or Brody, Marla worried about the next hour they'd spend in some of the more questionable establishments of the city.

She registered her sister's chatter, but none of the words resonated. She was on a mission. "Molly, hit that bar on the east side of the street. Mitzi, take one on the west. I'll check out the casino by the river a block away." The dark alley leading to the casino looked ominous, but she had her pepper spray and her cell phone flashlight, so she felt okay. What she hadn't told the girls was that she was also carrying a compact pistol in her bag, courtesy of Cooter. She'd found it under his pillow when she'd slept in his bed. "Stay in this general vicinity. Don't stray off and keep your phones handy."

"Right. Be careful," Mitzi warned. Always the practical one. "We don't know what we're getting into."

"Of course." Molly flashed a mischievous grin. "But danger is half the fun, right?"

"Right," Marla agreed, forcing a smile. "No, wrong. Keep it to business. Got it?"

Molly frowned.

Deep down, she felt more than determination—she honestly felt fear—whoever had hurt Cooter wouldn't hesitate to hurt them too, if they discovered them poking around. But her concern for Cooter and his whereabouts weighed heavy—even if he was dead, which she didn't want to believe. Plus, an urgency for answers haunted her. "Meet up again at the Pink Pig in thirty minutes. Don't linger if you're getting nowhere. Make it quick."

"Roger that." Mitzi headed west.

Molly turned toward her assigned bar.

The dark corners swallowed everything as Marla headed down the narrow street toward the river. People lurked in alleyways, their faces hidden inside hoodies and shadows. Homeless? Or drug dealers? Worse? She passed a couple of rundown bars and strip clubs, their neon lights casting a pulsing glow onto the garbage-strewn streets.

Taking a deep breath, she steeled herself for the next phase of their investigation. They were growing nearer; she could feel it in her bones. But as the shadows appeared to close in, she couldn't help but wonder if the darkness would consume them all before they found the truth.

Rounding a corner, the streetlights abruptly lit up the area, and she eased out a sigh of relief. The bright lights of the riverboat casino urged her forward. Before she entered, her phone binged with a text message.

Molly: *Hey. Guy here says he was at Cooter's on Sat. Saw a strange guy hanging around.*

Marla: *We've heard that before. Description?*

Molly: *Big, bald, tattoos on the back of his neck. Beard. Seems he asked Landry about Cooter's contract.*

Marla: *Interesting. Maybe a lead.*

Marla: *Can you get a name?*

Molly: *Will try.*

Marla: *Keep digging, Molls. Pink Pig in twenty.*

Molly: *Got it. Stay safe.*

Marla: *Always.*

Pushing through the front door to the casino, the rising and falling arpeggios of the slots, and the blinking lights consumed her. Marla felt a sudden urgency to get back to her sisters. Something wasn't right. Pulling out her phone again, she read over the string of text messages. No Mitzi.

Quickly scrolling for her sister's number, she pushed Mitzi's name and waited until the ringing went to voice mail. No answer. Turning on her heel, she headed back up the dark alley. They'd agreed to keep in touch and always answer a call or text. No word meant something was wrong.

Her stomach clutched.

Chapter Six

The lights inside the Pig Pen flickered erratically, buzzing like a swarm of drunken fireflies. Marla cruised through the bar assigned to Mitzi with no luck. Wrinkling her nose at the stale beer stench, she kept an eye out for both sisters as she pushed her way inside the crowded BBQ joint-slash-bar. She was early, she knew, but still hoped they'd surface soon.

Please be here.

She eyed the stage at the back of the place through a smoky aura. Her gaze scanned the picnic tables full of people and food up front, and the high-top bar tables to the left of the stage, and the crowded bar area to the right. If this was the underbelly of Shreveport's music scene, it was a far cry from Cooter's warmly lit biker bar.

But they were here for answers, not ambiance.

"Well, this place is charming." Mitzi's voice wafted over her shoulder.

Marla spun, her jaw tight, and caught her sister's eye. "Oh, my God. I thought you were in trouble."

"Why?"

"Because you didn't chime in on the texts."

Mitzi shrugged. "Because I was busy?"

"Hey girls. I made it. Twenty minutes. I think that's a record."

Marla and Mitzi stared at Molly.

"What?"

"I'm always late."

"Right." Marla shook her head. "Let's find a seat and share intel."

"There are three seats at the bar," Mitzi offered.

Marla spotted the three empty barstools. "Grab them." Sitting at the bar had advantages and disadvantages. She mused over the insanity of it all as she strode behind her sisters, making a beeline to the seats. An advantage was that bartenders talk. The disadvantage was, there were also a lot of listening ears.

They snagged the seats. Marla zeroed in on the bartender, whose stained apron unfortunately matched the grime on the bar top.

"What can I get you ladies?" he asked, eyes roving.

Marla leaned forward. "Information." She was not about to waste time.

The bartender's smile faded. "Not sure I can help with that."

"Oh, I think you can." Marla held his gaze. "We're looking into the accident involving Cooter Haines a couple of nights ago."

The guy stiffened. "You cops?"

Mitzi shook her head. "No. We're friends."

His gaze scanned all three sisters. "Well, yeah. I don't know nothing about that."

"Now why don't I believe you?" Molly said, voice sweet as honey.

Marla hid a smile. Molly could charm a confession out of anyone when she put her sweet, southern belle mind to it.

The bartender shifted, glancing around. "Look, I don't want trouble. Things happen around here, no questions asked. That's the code."

Marla slapped her hand on the bar, a twenty-dollar bill peeking out from underneath. "Well, we're asking questions. Cooter was family." The words tumbled out fiercely, surprising her. When had she started thinking of him like that?

The bartender glanced at the twenty, chuckled, then held up his hands. "Look. I ain't talking for that, so either order a drink or go sit somewhere else."

Marla glanced at her sisters. They were just getting started, and she wasn't leaving. "Order up, sisters," she told them. For Cooter, they'd search every seedy bar in Louisiana if they had to, and if drinking came with it, so be it.

"Gin and tonic here," Mitzi called out.

"I'll have a beer. Whatever is on tap," Marla told him.

"Got anything fruity with an umbrella?" Molly queried.

The guy behind the bar shot her a look.

"Okay then," Molly reneged. "Vodka. Dirty."

He snickered. "Coming up, ladies."

A cacophony of conflicting tunes and drunken laughter assaulted her ears as she looked away from the bartender and out into the bar again. Her sisters flanked her, their determination palpable.

When she looked back, she saw Molly leaning over the bar, her cleavage sparkly, like she'd glittered her girls up, staring into the bartender's eyes.

"Hey, handsome. I know you don't want to talk, but you say you know Cooter?"

"Sure. Hell of a drummer. Shame what happened." He placed her vodka in front of her.

"Did you hear anything about a new drummer in town? Someone who might've had a problem with him?" she asked, leaning closer, her V-neck top gapping.

The bartender took a long look, then finished with Mitzi's gin. "Can't say I did. But the Skull Bone manager was acting shifty around that time. Might be worth lookin' into." He lifted his gaze to peer into Mitzi's eyes, placing her drink in front of her. "But you didn't hear that from me. You got that?"

"Of course."

"Um-hmm." Molly circled a water ring on the bar with her manicured forefinger. "Hey," she said softly, "You know a guy who hangs out here sometimes? Big, bald head. Some tattoos on his neck?"

The bartender threw back his head and laughed. "Look around. See anyone who matches that description?"

The women humored him and glanced about. When they turned back, Marla found her beer on the bar. Finally. She took a sip.

Molly sucked in a slow breath. "Oh, I know." She ran a lazy finger around the rim of her martini glass. "This guy is real tall. He might be associated with Rick Landry, you know, the Skull Bone manager. You mentioned him. Ring a bell?"

He hesitated and swiped at the wet ring on the bar with a towel.

"Look," Mitzi added. "Cooter's accident hit us all hard. We're just some girls trying to find out what happened to our friend."

"Alright," the guy relented, his expression softening. "I heard some whispers about a guy who had it out for Cooter. Wanted his spot in the band. But I don't know much else."

Molly shimmied a little and leaned closer. His gaze went to her sparkly boobs.

Marla rolled her eyes. Men were so shallow.

"Word is," he went on, "that Landry had gotten the band into some deep financial trouble. Sloppy contracts and booked shows they lost money on. Cooter was expensive, or so I've heard. Damn, he was the best drummer in five states, so he should be. The scuttlebutt was that this new guy was cheaper."

"So this dude, the other drummer, was new in town?"

The bartender studied her. "Yes, I think that's right."

Marla and her sisters exchanged a look. This was the truth behind Cooter's death? Some new guy wanted Cooter's job, so he runs him off the road? Seemed too cruel, too unfair, too...simple.

Too stupid a reason to kill someone. There had to be more to this.

"You know this drummer's name?" Marla asked, her jaw tight with determination.

The bartender shook his head. "Haven't heard it mentioned," he replied, his voice low. "But I know several of the guys who play with Skull Bone hang out at a certain pool hall downtown. Harry's place, the locals call it. But the sign out front says, 'Get a Cue, Harry's Pool and Burgers.' You might poke around there, but seriously, be careful."

"Cute. Thanks." Marla placed a hundred-dollar bill on the bar. "For the drinks. Keep the change."

Turning to her sisters, she whispered, "Let's get out of here. We need to take a breath and regroup, then check out this pool hall."

* * *

The Shreveport night air clung to Marla's skin like wet silk as she and her sisters huddled around the hood of her jeep, their phones casting eerie blue glows on their faces. The time was approaching midnight, and the bars were more crowded than ever. Music throbbed from each of the establishments on music row. Streetlights flickered overhead, painting the cracked asphalt with disturbing shadows.

Glancing about, she scanned the area, a sneaking feeling of being watched bugging her.

"Okay," Mitzi began, scrolling through her phone, "There are theories all over social media about what happened to Cooter. I met this guy in the bar earlier who claims he saw Cooter there a couple of days before the accident, arguing with someone."

Marla studied her. "Makes no sense. Cooter was usually at his own bar every evening. What time was this?"

"Not sure. But there's footage from the bar's camera. I lured that out of the owner. I'll send you the link in text."

"Good lead," Marla said, her fingers flying over her own screen as she searched screen shots she'd taken of police records. "Looks like Landry has a history of financial problems. Maybe that's motive enough?"

"And he wants Cooter's bar," Molly added.

Marla nodded. "True. We need to remember that."

"And according to the bartender, Cooter was expensive."

Clicking the link Mitzi sent, her eyes scanned the grainy surveillance footage. The sense of being watched still gnawed at her, but she shook it off, focusing on the task at hand. She spotted a guy who could be Cooter, but she couldn't say that for sure. He seemed to be definitely arguing with another guy— beard, bald, and tall—with animated gestures. Then the tall guy abruptly turned and snuck out the back door, leaving Cooter standing there. "Girls, look at this," she said, pointing at the screen.

"Who's that?" Molly asked, squinting at the blurry image.

"Can't tell," Marla admitted, "but something about that guy is familiar. And the way he paused and stared at the other guy—

who could be Cooter—well, all I can say is it wasn't a good stare. We need to find out who he is. Let's head back to that bar you were in earlier, Mitzi. Think you can find the guy again who gave you this footage?"

"Sure thing, if he's still there. If not, he texted me the video, so I have his number."

"Great. Let's go. This street corner is giving me the creeps." Marla urged her sisters down the sidewalk toward the light, but she couldn't shake the feeling that they were being followed. Her heart raced, adrenaline pumping through her veins.

They passed a man in a hoodie, his face obscured, approaching them in a sloppy swagger.

Molly whispered. "Let's move across the street."

The girls took a sudden turn into the empty street.

"Hey!" A gravelly voice called out.

"Don't look back," Marla warned. "Keep going."

"Hey! What the hell, ladies? Can't you give a guy a minute?"

Marla looked over her shoulder. "Get lost, loser."

"Whoa. Kinda bitchy aren't you?" Out of the corner of her eye, she saw him step hurriedly into the street. "You think you can intimidate me?" He called after them.

Marla's heart hammered in her chest as she fought to remain calm. She turned, hurtling toward him, her hand nestled into the side pocket of her purse, fingers curled around the Equalizer. "Look," she said, trying to sound confident, "I have no problem defending myself, so back off, dude."

She had years of kickboxing under her belt and a self-defense class or two in her past. Plus, she worked out regularly and figured she was in much better shape than this pasty doughboy.

"Is that so?" The man lunged, but Marla sidestepped him, using her momentum to shove him several steps backward, wrench his arm behind him, and press his face into the brick wall. For good measure, she pushed the snub of her gun against his neck.

"My God, Marla!" Mitzi shrieked.

"I'm calling 9-1-1!" Molly yelled.

"Great." Marla shoved the pistol deeper.

"You're crazy, woman," he hissed.

"Who are you? Who *sent* you?"

"Nobody and nobody, bitch."

God, she hated that word, and he'd used it twice now. "You're on thin ice, dude. Watch it."

"You know I could take you in two seconds flat."

"Oh, really? Right." She twisted his arm tighter, and he yelped. "Stay the hell away from us," she warned, pushing back and stepping several steps away. He faced her. She kept the pistol pointed straight at his heart, her stance firm. "Get out of here. Go on. And leave us alone."

"Fine," he growled, rubbing his shoulder. "But poking around like you three are... It's a good way to end up dead."

"Is that a threat?"

"Call it whatever you want."

Abruptly, Mitzi raced forward. "Who the hell are you and why are you tailing us?" She reached for his hoodie and tugged it back off his head. The guy from the video? Maybe.

"Hey!" The guy batted at Mitzi's hand. He lunged.

Marla cocked her gun and took two steps closer. "Don't touch my sister," she growled.

The guy threw up his hands in defeat. "Not touching her."

"I've seen you somewhere before. You know Cooter Haines?"

"You know you shouldn't play with guns unless you plan to use them."

Marla cocked the pistol and pointed it in his face. "Don't give me an excuse."

"You're fucking crazy." He turned and ran into the shadows.

Marla lowered her gun and exhaled.

"Let's get out of here," Molly urged, tugging at her arm.

They didn't linger long, rushing across the street. None of them spoke until they reached the next block and brighter streetlights.

"I didn't know you had a gun," Molly whispered, leaning close.

Mitzi halted, her eyes round. "Me either!"

Shaking off their comments, Marla said, "I didn't want you to know. I found it in Cooter's bedroom last night."

"Do you know how to use that thing?"

She stopped then, in front of the bar, and turned. "Yes. It's Cooter's. He taught me how a while back. We used to go to the shooting range together."

"Oh."

Molly arched a brow. "Would you have shot that guy?"

Lowering her gaze, she peered directly into Molly's eyes. "If he came after any of the three of us, you better believe I would squeeze that trigger and not think about it again."

Molly held her gaze and let out a slow breath. "Wow. You are a badass."

"Did either of you get a good look at him?"

"Not really," Mitzi said. "It happened too fast and there were shadows."

"Me neither," Molly added.

Marla took Molly's arm. "Let's go inside. I feel safer in there than out here on the street."

"Agreed."

Her pulse raced as she walked into the dimly lit bar, Molly

and Mitzi flanking her. A sense of dread washed over her, but she brushed it off.

"Let's ask around while we're here," Marla suggested. "But be careful, okay? And no one leaves unless we all do."

"Got it," Molly quipped, heading to a group huddled in the corner.

"Same here," Mitzi responded, making her way to the bar.

Marla slowly approached a tall, tattooed man leaning against the wall, his eyes fixed on the stage.

"Good band," she said, looking forward.

She sensed him slowly angle her way. "They do okay."

"I don't think I know them."

"The Boys and Billy Joe, they call themselves."

Marla nodded. "I like the Skull Bone, myself." She looked at him. Tall. Bald. Did he have tattoos on his neck? Hard to see in the darkened room.

"Thought I recognized you." He crossed his arms and pressed his back against the wall. "You hang out at Deadheads."

"I do. Did. Kind of hard to go back there right now."

"Yeah. Too bad about Cooter."

"You knew him?"

"Knew of him."

"Know anything about his accident?"

The man looked down his nose, his lip curled into a sneer. "Why would I know anything about that?"

She shrugged, nonchalantly. "Just trying to find out who ran him off the road."

"And why would you be coming in here and zeroing in on me?"

Marla met his gaze. "To be honest, you're not special, dude. I'm asking everyone."

He held her gaze for several ticks of her heart. She knew that, because her heart beat so loudly at his stare, she was sure he could hear it, too. Finally, he bit out, "Word of advice. Mind your own business, sweetheart."

"It is my business. Cooter was my old man."

His face froze. "Then you better get your ass back to Deadhead, where you'll be safe. You're in the wrong part of town to be sneaking around asking questions. Got it? You and your sisters need to hightail it home before it's too late."

Ending the conversation, he turned his back and stalked away.

You and your sisters. Marla let out a pent-up breath. *Before it's too late.*

She moved away from the fringes, glancing about for her sisters.

Finally, she found them near the entrance. "Anything?" she asked, her voice laced with frustration.

"Nothing useful," Molly admitted, shaking her head. "Just a bunch of dead ends."

"Same here," Mitzi added, her brow furrowed in concern. "You?"

"Maybe. I want to process it. Let's go back to Deadhead." The guy at the stage was right. She felt safer there. He knew who they were. Not good. The word about them was out. "Let's regroup and try again tomorrow."

"I like that plan," Molly said, stepping out into the cool night air.

"Wait. I thought we were going to check out the pool hall? Harry's place? Get a cue?"

Marla contemplated that for only a second, glancing down the street. Should they just go on and do that tonight? Suddenly, the guy from the stage stepped out of the alley and onto the sidewalk. Casting his gaze toward her, he held her stare for a moment, as if in warning, then headed for a bike parked on the street.

"No. Let's head back to see if Luke uncovered anything tonight. Harry's tomorrow night if we need to."

Maybe they wouldn't need to. Maybe things would be resolved by then. She could only hope.

Mitzi glanced at her watch. "You know, I would love to go back to The Deadhead, but Ken got home from New Orleans a couple of hours ago. I should probably go grab some cuddle time with my hubby."

Molly nodded and yawned, the back of her hand to her mouth. "Yeah, and I need to pick up the kids early in the morning from Mom—she has plans for the day. I should get some sleep."

"That's fine. Tomorrow. Let's say afternoon, at one o'clock, at The Deadhead. I'll check in with Luke tonight, then call it a day. Maybe I'll sleep at Cooter's. I don't know."

"Works for me."

"I'll get a sitter for the kids."

"All right then. Be safe."

They scattered, moving toward their vehicles. Marla held back beside her Jeep until both her sisters were inside their locked cars, safe and sound. Then got into her vehicle and headed for Deadheads.

* * *

The dim lighting of The Deadhead cast eerie shadows across the walls, illuminating the vintage concert posters of Cooter's favorite bands. Marla took a deep breath and steeled herself, her heart uneasy as she pushed open the creaky door. Her eyes darted around the biker bar, searching for any trace of the man who had claimed a piece of her heart.

It seemed so surreal that Cooter wasn't standing behind that bar.

She still had a difficult time believing he wasn't coming back to her.

Marla Newberry was known around Carrington to never back down from a challenge, and she wouldn't back down now. The mystery surrounding Cooter's disappearance consumed every waking thought. She was determined to find out if he was dead or alive—only seeing his deceased body would satisfy her that he wasn't coming back.

The familiar scent of stale beer and smoke filled her nostrils as she wove through the crowd. It was well after midnight and the place was still hopping.

"Hey, Marla!" The voice rose above the noise.

"Luke." She headed his way.

Leaning against the bar, he wiped down a glass with a towel. One corner of his mouth turned up as his gaze followed her—but something else lurked beneath the surface that Marla couldn't quite put her finger on. Had he found out something?

"Hey." She tossed him a tight smile as she approached.

"The girls with you?"

"No. They went home. We will regroup tomorrow."

"Any news on your end?"

"Maybe. I'm still gathering my thoughts. You?"

"Eh, not really. I'm mulling it over too."

Eyeing him, Marla wondered what he had uncovered. "I may need your help, Luke. Can you meet us here tomorrow at one? We want to make a plan for tomorrow night."

"Anything for you." His voice dropped an octave as he leaned closer, slightly invading her personal space.

Marla's cheeks heated, a mixture of surprise and discomfort. The walls of the bar seemed to close in, a little.

"Get you a drink?" Luke's voice was low and inviting.

"Uh, sure," she replied hesitantly, her gaze flickering over his face as she tried to gauge his intentions. She appreciated his support, but the thought of anything beyond friendship made her stomach churn with unease. "Just a Coke, please. It's late and I need to drive home tonight."

"You could stay here again."

She shook her head. Suddenly, that felt like a dreadful idea. "No. I need to go home."

"Whatever works for you."

"Yes. I would like that Coke now." Her mouth was suddenly dry as a bone.

"Coming right up." Luke winked, turning away.

What were these conflicting emotions swirling between them? He wasn't coming on to her. Was he?

No. They were friends. That was all.

Right?

As Marla watched him go, she couldn't help but feel a little guilty. Luke was a good friend—but now, when she needed a friend to lean on more than ever, falling into his waiting arms wasn't the answer. No denying that the handsome bartender had always been there for her and Cooter, but this new intensity in his eyes was something she couldn't quite shake.

She'd never been one to bow to a man's affections, and she wasn't about to start now. Keeping Luke at arm's length—pure friendship—was all she could offer.

Her connection to Cooter, however dead or alive he might be, still bound her heart tightly.

"Here's that Coke." Luke's hand grazed her fingers as he handed her the glass, causing her to flinch ever so slightly.

"Thanks." Her gaze locked onto the condensation on the glass.

"Look, Marla," Luke began, his voice taking on a serious tone. "I know things are tough right now, and I'm here for you. But I need to know that you're not just using me as a crutch."

Whoa. Her gaze shot up to meet his. That was a turn she hadn't expected.

"Absolutely not, Luke," she stammered. "I'd never do that. You're a good friend and I would never take advantage of that fact." Is that what he thought of her? How had she misconstrued his earlier actions?

"Fair enough," he replied, his expression softening. "Just remember that I'm here if you need me."

"Thank you," she whispered, touched by his understanding, but also puzzled at their exchange. Suddenly, she was confused.

Time to change the subject.

"You dig up any news about Cooter tonight?"

Luke's brow furrowed. "Nothing concrete. But we'll find out what happened to him, I promise."

"Thanks," Marla murmured, appreciating his support.

"You know…" Luke rested a hand over hers on the bar. "You can count on me, right?"

"Of course."

The way his fingers lingered just a mite too long, however, didn't go unnoticed. She gave him another tight-lipped smile before slipping her hand away, her focus returning to her one and only quest—finding out the truth about Cooter. She glanced to her left.

"I see a friend over there." She lied. "I'm going to go say hello, and then head home and get some sleep. See you tomorrow afternoon. Bye Luke."

"See you tomorrow, Marla."

She waved, not turning around, and left.

Chapter Seven

The hour drive back to Carrington had tired her out more than she realized. Normally, she liked the drive —it provided a sense of space and time away from the bar to think about things. But tonight—probably because of the late hour and maybe that it had been an endless day—her emotions were drained and her physical body too.

They'd tried their darnedest to find some clues, identify some sort of motivation for Cooter's accident and the anger between him and Landry, but the results were few.

"You'll figure it out," she mumbled to herself. "You always do."

Never so happy to pull into her apartment complex, she parked as close to her unit as she could, quickly headed toward her apartment door to unlock it, and slipped inside. Once there, she dropped her purse and keys on the sofa and headed to her bedroom.

Stripping out of her clothing, she let them fall in a heap on the floor, then slipped between the cool covers of her bed.

* * *

The smoky haze of Cooter's bar surrounded Marla as she nursed her whiskey sour. Music and laughter swirled as she glanced around the place, looking for him. Where was he? He was always behind the bar, ready to serve customers.

Cooter. Her Cooter.

On stage, the band's bluesy rock filtered through the fog—she didn't know their name, and wondered if this was their first time at Deadhead—but she barely registered the music over the circling voices in her head.

She swirled the amber liquid, staring into memories. Cooter grinning as he mixed her favorite drink, his gravelly voice whispering in her ear. The brush of his hand on her back as he passed by, sending titillating spirals down her spine—a tease of things to come later that night. The way his eyes lit up when she walked in the door. She loved that tenderness beneath his gruff biker exterior, the tenderness he saved just for her.

Now he was missing, and Marla was left grasping at ghosts. She blinked back tears, anger and grief battling inside. Whoever did this was going to pay. She would find them, no matter what it took. The truth was out there somewhere in the shadows, and she was going to drag it into the light.

The ice clinked as she drained the last sip. Slamming the glass down with resolve, she stood. A dizzying sensation seized her. Cooter's face floated before her. Had she had one too many whiskey sours? Or was something else going on?

Suddenly, the heavy wooden door to the bar swung open, casting a sliver of light across the darkened bar. Marla turned to see a familiar silhouette standing in the entrance.

"Luke?"

He entered, the door falling closed behind him with a thud that ricocheted through the cluttered spaces of her mind. His boots pounded on the worn floorboards as he approached, his gaze locked on hers.

"Hey there." He stepped up directly in front of her.

"Hey."

"I loved him too, you know," Luke said. "Like a brother. And I miss him."

Marla met his gaze and held it steady. Why would he say that? There was something deeper in his words, an unspoken truth hanging in the smoky air. He was hurting, too. Why hadn't she thought of that?

But something else... Something inside her. A spark of connection, perhaps, a temptation to give in to the solace he offered.

That wasn't wise. Was it? No.

Of course, not.

Guilt gnawed at her insides. Cooter was missing, and her heart was already being pulled in another direction. She wasn't ready, wasn't free to explore those feelings for Luke, or anyone else.

Was she?

What's happening to my heart? At once, she felt sad and overwhelmed.

"I know," she whispered, offering him a weak smile. He meant well. But ghosts still haunted her heart. One ghost.

Turning away, she sat again and stared into her empty glass, wishing it could offer some answers.

When the barstool next to her creaked, she jumped. Movement settled in beside her, drawing her gaze away from her drink. Cooter sat there—as beautiful and as alive as ever—a wistful smile playing on his lips. His rugged charm never failed to draw her in.

"Evening, darlin'," he said. "Fancy seeing you here." His wicked smile was nearly her undoing.

"Cooter," she gasped. Her breath caught in her throat; her heart jumped in her chest. She'd seen Cooter's spirit before, but having him here now, in the bar, with Luke standing just on the other side, felt dangerously complicated.

Was he dead or alive?

He sure looked alive. Nothing like how he'd looked before when he came to her.

Was this real, or was she dreaming?

A mist of uncertainty and melancholy engulfed her.

"Cooter," she murmured. "What are you doing here?"

He smirked. "Missed that pretty face of yours, hon."

Warmth rose in her cheeks. The man could make her blush like a schoolgirl. She snuck a glance at Luke, but he showed no reaction to Cooter's presence.

"We need to talk." Cooter leaned closer, his playful tone turning serious. "I don't like where things seem to be headed with you and Luke."

Marla bristled. "Nothing happening there, Cooter. Not on my end."

His eyes, rather ghostly now, flashed with jealousy. But before he could respond, Luke cut in.

"Everything okay, Marla?" he asked gently. "You seem kind of distant suddenly."

Nothing is okay.

She opened her mouth, then closed it again. How could she explain any of this to Luke? She didn't understand it herself.

"I'm fine," she said finally. "Just thinking about Cooter."

Cooter snorted. He reached out, as if to caress her face, but Marla trembled and dodged his touch. How would she react if he actually touched her? She wanted to fall into his arms right now, let him warm her body with his every caress, but what would that look like if he really wasn't there?

Or if she were the only one who could see him?

Which had to be, right? Because Luke hadn't acknowledged his presence.

Could no one see him but her?

Luke leaned in. "You're shivering. Are you cold? Here..." He took off his jacket and draped it around her shoulders.

Marla blinked in surprise. "Luke, you don't have to...."

"I want to," he said. Was she imagining the husky note in his voice? "I'll always be here for you, Marla. Whatever you need."

Cooter sprang from his barstool. "Okay, that's enough. I'm not gonna sit here and watch some living Romeo put the moves on my girl."

Marla's cheeks flamed. "Cooter, stop." Her voice broke on the last word.

Luke's forehead creased. "Marla? What's going on?"

She hesitated, tears stinging her eyes. She didn't want this. Hadn't encouraged it. Why was this suddenly a love triangle that was becoming a powder keg of emotion? One she did not know how to defuse? Or wanted?

The stale beer smell and bluesy guitar wafted between them, making everything feel dreamlike and disconnected.

Dreamlike and disconnected.

"It's complicated, but...." she finally said.

"But what?" Luke prodded.

Ghostly Cooter muttered under his breath.

"I still see him, Luke. I see Cooter."

Luke's eyes widened. "His ghost? You mean...?"

"I don't know what he is. Ghost? Real? He's here right now, sitting on that barstool and glaring daggers at you. I know it sounds crazy."

"I love you, Marla."

No. No, no, no. She stood and backed away. "No, Luke. Don't go there."

He followed her, cupping her elbows in his palms. "Give me a chance?" He slanted closer, angling toward her lips.

No! She pushed back.

Cooter drifted closer, putting his body between her and Luke, his voice softening. "Darlin', you know I'll always love you."

She felt lost in his eyes. *Cooter. Oh, Cooter. I miss you so.*

The blues guitarist on stage slid into a melancholy solo, underscoring her turmoil. Cooter suddenly faded.

"Cooter! No! Don't leave me!"

Marla jerked, sitting straight up in her bed. "Cooter!"

Gasping in breath after breath, she stared blindly into the night. Beads of sweat popped up on her forehead, the nape of her neck damp.

A glance at the old digital clock beside her bed told her she'd barely slept an hour. Her breath shallow and coming way too quickly, she steeled herself against the dizziness suddenly swallowing up her head.

Slow breaths, Marla.

She needed to calm her heart rate.

Needed to push thoughts of Luke out of her head.

Needed to hold on to that feeling of loving Cooter.

Dream. Damn dream.

Once she'd calmed, she looked into the dark, staring at the foot of her bed. "Cooter? Are you out there? I need you."

Nothing but emptiness echoed back.

Chapter Eight

Marla stared into the depths of her coffee. She'd arrived at The Deadhead earlier than her sisters, going over the events of the previous night. Having not slept well—her head reeling with the dream of Cooter—she was groggy and tired. Her thoughts were also consumed with the nagging feeling she was missing something important. She glanced over at Luke, who was busy behind the bar, and wondered if he might have any fresh insights.

While she was leery of approaching him, she knew he cared for Cooter and wanted answers as much as she did.

Still, his behavior last night had rather discombobulated her. He'd bounced between hot and cold—like he was coming on to her one minute and putting her at arm's length the next. The exchange they'd had was difficult to grasp, and things weren't any clearer today.

The dream didn't help.

But she had to trust Luke. He was the only one who really seemed to want to help—besides her sisters and Brody.

Hm. When would Brody get back from New Orleans? She'd ask Molly.

It was a slow afternoon. A couple of guys played pool over in the corner. A woman she'd seen there a time or two sat at the end of the bar eating a hamburger. Southern rock piped through the overhead speakers. This place was comfort, but she wasn't sure it would ever feel quite the same.

Honestly, she wondered if she was too tired to head back to the bars tonight. It was the plan she and her sisters had discussed the night before—but now, she wondered if it was a good idea. The scene with the guy on the street, with her pulling out her pistol, worried her. She'd been lucky. The guy could have easily turned the tables on her, but he didn't. She had to wonder why. It was like he was letting her get away with it.

Maybe he, too, was a warning—like the others.

"Hey," Luke called out, leaning into the bar. "You need something more than coffee? Something to perk you up?" He sat a whiskey sour on the bar in front of her.

She stared at it and immediately thought of her dream. Her gaze jerked up at Luke.

"Can't fool you, can I?" Marla forced a smile. "I'm just... I'm still trying to wrap my head around... Well, everything."

"Cooter?" Luke asked, concern etched on his face.

"And some stuff that happened last night." *Stuff you should probably know about. Stuff in my dream you shouldn't know about. Why the whiskey sour?*

This is weird.

"Want to talk?"

She eyed him, taking in his serious demeanor. He'd been great to her through all of this. Now was not the time to doubt him. He might be teasing the waters a bit, trying to move in on her romantically, but she had no reason to think he was not being honest about Cooter. "I think going back to music row tonight is not such a good idea. Maybe it's time to give it up."

Luke shifted, leaning in on his elbows. "Why? What happened?"

She blew out a breath. "Someone is onto us—my sisters and me. We were followed, and a guy approached us on the street. Also, I got a stark warning from another dude telling us to back off. Actually, it seemed like everywhere we went, someone told us to give it up and go home."

"So, Cooter's accident is a touchy subject in the bar scene downtown."

"Definitely."

"Like, maybe they know something, but don't want to give up the details."

"Exactly."

"Interesting."

"Yes." Marla sighed. "But I really don't want to give up, Luke. I still don't believe that he's gone. There is more to this than what we see on the surface."

"Actually..." Luke hesitantly glanced about and lowered his voice. "I heard something this morning that might interest you."

"Go on," Marla urged, her curiosity piqued.

"Now," his gaze shifted back and forth again, "I have no proof of this, but rumor has it someone spotted Cooter on music row downtown a couple of nights ago." Luke's voice was barely audible above the din of the bar. "And since they did not find his body, people are saying he's still alive out there somewhere."

"What?"

"Yeah. And there is speculation that the accident never happened. That Cooter staged it all, faking his death, in order to get out of paying some sort of debt to someone."

"Are you serious?" Marla scoffed, her brow furrowing skeptically. "That's ridiculous. How could he get all the way from the accident to Shreveport, injured no less, with no one knowing? Plus, what about his bike?"

79

"Beats me. We found the damaged bike," Luke admitted with a shrug. "But if there's even the slightest chance he's still alive, don't you think it's worth looking into?"

Marla's chest stiffened. Suddenly, her heart felt battered and weary. She was torn between hope and the crushing weight of reality. Her practical side wanted to dismiss the notion outright, but another part couldn't help but cling to the possibility of Cooter being alive.

But what about the visions?

I have to go back. I have to know.

"Yes. Cooter is worth it."

Luke grinned.

"The girls will be here soon. We are going to Harry's pool hall because we've heard the Skull Bone guys hang out there. Come with us?"

Pushing away from the bar, Luke stood upright. "I'll see if I can get away—I'd have to call in another bartender, so I don't know. With Cooter gone, there aren't many people I trust to run the place. I'll find you."

"Text me." Marla nodded. "The only plan so far is the pool hall. If that changes, I'll let you know."

"Great." Luke glanced up. "Ah, I see one of your partners in crime now."

Molly slipped into the seat beside her. "Hey sis," she said, her eyes bright despite the late night before. "Mitzi's behind me. We might have a lead on the case."

Marla straightened, the fog in her mind clearing. "Oh?"

"Brody called earlier."

"Great. I was going to ask you when he was coming back."

Grinning, Molly continued. "Late tonight or early in the morning. He's wrapping things up down there. But listen to this —he said one of his street contacts saw a guy matching the description of that other drummer out back at Cooter's the night things went haywire."

"The rival drummer?" Marla whispered.

"He was here that night," Luke interrupted. "Yeah, I've seen him around lately."

The women stared at him. "What?"

Shrugging, Luke went on. "Didn't know it was something to consider. The guy was with Landry. But now that I think about it, maybe he is the reason Landry cut Cooter's contract."

"You think?"

The look on Luke's face puzzled Marla. Like he was making stuff up on the fly.

Molly nodded. "Well. Brody's looking into it now. If we can place him at the scene, it could give us an actual suspect."

Marla's pulse quickened, her detective instincts kicking in. After days of dead ends, maybe they were finally getting a break.

"You two all rested and ready for the day?" Mitzi joined them, sitting to her right.

Sighing, Molly picked at a fingernail. "I forgot I had a nail appointment and had to cancel. I'm sad."

Marla rolled her eyes. "You'll live."

"But it's chipped." Molly held up a lavender painted forefinger.

"Good God," Mitzi quipped. "It's just a nail."

"Well, I know that, but I hate being uneven!" She put up her other forefinger.

Mitzi reached across in front of Marla. "Give it to me."

"What?"

"Give me your stupid finger!"

Molly pushed the unchipped finger forward. Mitzi pulled a pocketknife out of her purse and scratched at the polish on the nail. "There. You're even. Now, can we get on with things?"

Drawing back, Molly pouted. "Fine."

Marla laid her head down on the bar and closed her eyes. Some days with these two were just too much.

"We should probably check out that lead," Molly said.

"What lead?"

Marla raised her head and looked at Mitzi. "We can explain in the car. Who is driving?"

Molly volunteered.

But did they really want to head into the seedy underbelly of Shreveport's music scene in Molly's lavender Cadillac?

"I don't think so. Let's take my jeep."

"Fine."

Marla ignored her little sister's sulk. As they rushed from the bar, Marla steeled herself, pushing aside ghosts and heartache.

* * *

Her boots clicked on the pavement as the trio approached the graffiti-covered pool hall. The neon sign above the door flickered, *Get a Cue*, it said, cast eerie shadows on the street. This was their last attempt in their quest for answers, she hoped, a knot forming in her stomach.

"Ready?" Mitzi turned, her hand lingering on the door handle. Molly's eyes darted around, as if taking in every detail.

Two men stepped out of the doors and passed them with a cocky sway.

"Wait." Marla tugged her sisters aside. "Let's go over the plan one more time. Molly?"

"Okay. I am covering the bar. My boobs are glittery and I've got ample cleavage. Bartenders look and talk. I'm asking about seeing Cooter a few nights ago. I'm to use my feminine wiles to lure away info. Then meet up front in thirty minutes."

Nodding, Marla turned to Mitzi. "And?"

"I'm on bouncer detail and other customers. A floater. I'll get a drink and cruise the tables, see if I can distract the guy at the door a little, in order to squeeze some Cooter siting info from him. I'll wait near the door for you all in thirty. If I can snag a table there, I will."

"Good."

"And you, Marla?"

"I've got the Skull Bones, wherever they are—playing pool or drinking in the back. Since they probably will recognize me as Cooter's girlfriend, hopefully I have an angle. Time will tell. I'll be back at the front at the designated time."

"We got this."

"Let's do it." Marla's voice sounded steady despite the unease creeping through her veins. She inhaled deep and rechecked the gun in her boot. She'd borrowed Cooter's elastic ankle holster and having never worn one before, realized it was a little annoying—but she was glad to have the gun in a place where she couldn't grab it too easily, but also within reach should she need it. Besides, she wasn't carrying a purse tonight.

The low hum of conversation and the twang of a guitar greeted them inside. A haze of cigarette smoke hung in the air, and she squinted against the shadowy atmosphere. She scanned the room, identifying potential sources of information—a group huddled around the bar, random couples in booths and at tables, the bouncer standing inside the door to their left, and some men she recognized playing pool—some of the Skull Bone band.

"Alright, let's see what we can find," Marla suggested, her gaze locking onto the musicians. Molly and Mitzi nodded, moving towards their own targets.

As she approached the guys, she noticed their guarded expressions and tried to ignore the sinking feeling in her chest. She forced a smile and tried to sound casual. "Hey."

A tall guy with tattoo sleeves, and holding a pool cue, stopped what he was doing and stood up, eyeing her. "Playing a game here, hon. What you want?"

"Saw you guys at Deadhead last Saturday night."

One of the other guys stepped forward. "That was a good set. You in the audience?"

"At the bar. Yeah, I love to listen to you all."

"You're pretty much a regular there."

Her gaze bounced around the four men standing around the table. "Yeah. You could say that."

The guy with the cue leaned over the table, pointing the cue at a ball. "What's your question, hon. You're Cooter's old lady, right? Any news on him?"

Marla inhaled, then hissed out a quick breath. "Yeah. I'm Cooter's girlfriend. Just looking for info about what happened that night. Anyone help me out?"

Silence fell over the pool table, with only the occasional clink of glass breaking the tension. After a few passing seconds, one musician spoke up. "Look, we know nothing. And even if we did, we told everything we knew to the police."

The police? Why hadn't she thought to go there before now? Surely they have some intel they could share.

"Listen," Marla pressed. "I just want to find out what happened to my guy. If you know anything—"

"Sorry, can't help you."

Suddenly, she felt dismissed.

"RIP Cooter. Hope he died a swift death." They turned their backs and watched the guy with the cue break a triangle of balls.

Maybe she should just go for it. "Did you know there's a rumor going around that he's not dead?"

"Huh?" The cue guy lifted his gaze from the table.

"Yeah. Supposedly, he was spotted here, downtown, a few nights ago."

"No shit."

"Seriously. In fact, I believe it could be true, his body never being found and all. I just need to find out where he is, though, and why he's not contacting me. That worries me and makes me think something is going on. You got anything you can share?"

The men exchanged glances but didn't offer anything.

The tattooed guy set his pool cue on the table. "Look. If we could help you, we could. Only thing I can say at this point is that it ain't Landry, like so many people are saying. Landry was as shocked as the rest of us when Cooter came at him that night."

"And why did he do that? It was so out of the blue."

"You didn't know he got cut from the band?"

"I heard rumors but nothing concrete. He didn't tell me."

Cue guy nodded. "Landry cut him and gave his son the drummer gig." He glanced around to the other men. "His son, Jack, needed a job. We weren't too happy about that, but not a lot we could do. Cooter was a big draw. People would come from miles to hear him. Landry was an idiot."

Marla stared. The rival drummer was Landry's son? Her brain spun. "I don't get it."

"We don't either, for sure. All we know is that Jack Landry was in some kind of trouble out in California, and he came home. Maybe Landry was trying to keep him under his nose."

Marla thought there was more to it than that. She stepped closer. "Random question. Do you know why Landry would think he is going to take over Cooter's bar? He seems to think in time it will be his."

The band members looked at each other.

Cue guy shook his head. "Haven't a clue, hon. Sorry about that."

"No worries."

"Hell, I'm thirsty." He eyed her for a few seconds, then turned away. "Let's go in the back and get a beer, boys."

She stood there looking after them, realizing she was still no closer to finding the truth.

* * *

Mitzi and Molly sat together at a corner table near the front, their eyes scanning the room as they sipped their drinks. Sounds of clinking of glasses and the murmur of conversation filled the dimly lit bar. Marla was curious if her sisters had any success at all. Once the Skull Bone had abandoned her, there was little more she could do. To be honest, she felt a bit deflated.

Might be best to get the hell out of here, anyway.

Frustrated, she pulled out a chair and sat, her hands trembling.

"No one's talking," Mitzi told her. "They are either too scared or too loyal."

"Same here."

"I need booze." Marla glanced at the bar. "I got some info from the Skull Bone guys, though. I just don't know what to do with it."

Molly leaned forward. "What is it?"

"The new drummer? It's Landry's son. Also, the band guys think it surprised Landry when Cooter angrily approached him about cutting him from the band. I think the son is in on this, but I still can't figure out why and how."

Mitzi shrugged. "Maybe the son saw Cooter go after his dad, went off half-cocked, and chased after Cooter?"

"Instead of Cooter chasing Landry? Which is what I had assumed."

"Maybe."

Marla drummed her fingers on the table. "You know, we never went to the police to get their view on all of this."

"No," Molly said, "But Brody did, right? He had copies of all those reports in that box. Oh, and by the way, he's coming home later." Her smile lit up the gloom at the table.

"I'm happy for you," Marla said. "Do you all need another round?"

"I'm good," Molly said.

"Maybe another LIT in a few," Mitzi added.

"I can't decide if I want beer or something harder." Marla settled back into her chair.

Molly gave her a saucy grin. "Something harder is always better."

"You're a mess." Marla laughed. "But I love you."

"Backatcha, Sis."

She glanced at the bar again, then drummed her fingers on the table. "Man, I tell you, this is all weighing heavy on me, girls. Not sure I can do another night."

"Let's not give up yet," Molly said. "We'll find someone who's willing to share what they know."

"Right," Mitzi chimed in. "Besides, we've barely scratched the surface here."

"I know, but—"

"Drinks ladies?"

Marla looked up. A young woman with a nose ring and wearing a Guns & Roses T-shirt stood between her and Mitzi, balancing a tray of drinks. She began placing them on the table. "You read my mind?"

The woman smiled. "Compliments of the old dude at the bar." She ticked her head that way.

All three sisters looked. A mature gentleman wearing a red bandana on his head, a long gray pigtail trailing down his back, and a worn and seen-better-days leather biker jacket, turned and tipped his drink to the girls.

"Who is that?" Molly asked.

The server grinned. "Haven't a clue. First time I've seen him here. But drink up, ladies, it's a whiskey sour special, and it's on the house!"

Marla felt an obligation to the Willie Nelson looking dude, so she tipped her glass his way and smiled. He winked back.

Ugh. Last thing she wanted or needed was a pickup artist fawning over her. "Let's drink these and get out of here," she said.

"Wait." Mitzi placed her hand on Marla's arm. "See that guy over there by the door? I didn't hear everything he said, but he mentioned Cooter to the guy next to him."

"Really?" Marla's heart skipped a beat. "He doesn't look familiar at all."

"I know."

Molly sipped her drink, then patted the table. "Oh, he's leaving. Let's follow him."

"But we just got these drinks!"

"Chug 'em." Molly's chair screeched as she scooted back and stood. Tipping back her drink, she downed it like a pro, gave the old dude a thumbs up, then set the tumbler back on the table. "Let's go."

Mitzi swallowed hers as well.

Marla pulled back. "I don't know if I want to follow him, girls. I really want to leave."

Mitzi stood over her. "Then we'll leave, just as soon as we see where he is heading."

"And maybe we can ask him some questions." Molly grinned as she joined Mitzi.

"Well, shit. All right." Standing, Marla took a long drink of the whiskey sour. The bite of the whiskey lit her throat on fire. Damn, it was good, though. She turned toward her sisters.

"Hey lady. Hold up."

Marla angled back. The Skull Bone guys were behind her—the four guys she'd spoken to earlier—and moving closer. "Wait," she hollered out at her sisters. "Hold up a minute."

Halting, she gave the band her attention. "Yeah?"

The guy who had done all the talking earlier leaned closer. "Look, hon. Cooter was one of us. We're all mourning what happened to him in our own way. We want to see justice too. Just know if you need us, we'll come running. Got that? You're one of us too."

Right then, her throat started closing up, and she wondered if she was going to ugly sob right there in front of them all—but she didn't. "I can't tell you how much that means to me, you guys."

They all grinned, every one of them.

"We'll be watching out for you."

"Oh. Thank you."

Then they left. Enough said, apparently.

Marla rotated back to her sisters.

"Well, that was cool," Molly said.

Mitzi agreed. "I like those guys."

"Me, too."

"Let's get rolling." Mitzi took both her sister's arms and led them toward the door.

They left and Marla hesitated just outside the door, glimpsing a shadowy figure disappearing into the alley. Molly tugged her into the street. "So now you are chicken shit? Big, bad girl with a gun. What's up with you tonight?" Her laugh was a little giddy and weird, and Marla wondered if she'd had too much to drink.

"Come on." Mitzi's voice sounded hollow and echoe-y, as if it were coming up from a deep well.

"Fine." What did she have to be afraid of, anyway?

Suddenly, her world spun, and Marla struggled to stay upright. "What's...happening?"

"I don't feel so good...." Mitzi called out.

Through blurry eyes, Marla watched her sister fall to the street. "Mitz...."

Molly screeched.

Grasping for her sister's arm, she came up with air. She was going down too. A man's boots shuffled through her tunnel vision, followed by muffled voices. Shadowy figures approached and meandered in and out of her consciousness, their faces obscured by darkness.

Then everything went totally black.

Chapter Nine

Marla slowly regained consciousness, her head pounding with a dull ache. She lay on the floor, her cheek pressed against something cold and damp. *Concrete or stone?* It was difficult to tell or see. As her eyes adjusted, blinking into awareness, she realized she was in a dank, dreary place—a cellar, perhaps? A crack of streetlight jutted in from a high, boarded window across the way. Or maybe it was sunlight.

Either way, she'd been laying there for a while.

An annoying click sounded in her brain, echoing against the damp floor.

Tick. Tick. Tick.

Gloom pressed in like a physical weight, making it difficult to breathe. The room was chilly, the air thick with the scent of mildew and rot. Water dripped from somewhere, each drop echoing through the underground chamber.

Was that what she was hearing? Dripping?

No.

Tick. Tick. Tick.

Where are my sisters?

She attempted to push up but couldn't—her head heavy and woozy. Her arms were bound behind her, and apparently, her ankles too. Shit!

Panic rose in her chest, threatening to engulf her entirely. "Must've drugged us. Need to... Get out of here." Her voice sounded mumble-y in her head.

"Marla," a voice whispered. "You there?"

"Molly? Thank God." She pulled against her restraints. "You okay?"

"Been better," she grumbled. "You?"

"Same." Marla winced as fibers dug into her skin. "Mitzi?"

"Here," came the muffled reply. "I've had pleasanter experiences."

Marla attempted a weak chuckle. "We'll find a way out of this mess."

"I'm scared."

"Me too," Mitzi added. "I can barely see a thing."

Marla took a deep breath, forcing herself to stay calm. She surveyed the dark surroundings, looking for anything that could help them escape. Her eyes adjusting to the dim light, she surveyed the crumbling brick walls, old boxes, and rusty tools strewn haphazardly about. A single bulb with a very faint dingy glow hung from the ceiling, silhouetted by the sliver coming in from the cracked window.

Tick. Tick. Tick.

Molly's teeth chattered. "Where are we?"

"Not sure," Marla whispered. "An old warehouse maybe." She stared into the dark and added, "Do you all hear that?"

"Hear what?"

"Some sort of clicking, like a...."

"Like a clock ticking?" Mitzi offered.

A clock. Her brain went to the old yellow clock in the diner. "Yes. Ticking."

Tick. Tick. Tick.

Time's running out. But for what?

She pulled her wrists apart, trying to stretch the bindings around her hands. "I might work my hands out," she said.

"Me too. Mine are loose-ish."

Turning toward Mitzi's voice coming from her left, she tried to make out the outline of her sister in the dark. "Where's Molly?"

"Beside me," Mitzi answered.

"You're both to my left. Good. Keep trying to loosen your hands."

"If I can get my hands out," Molly said, "I can get my phone. It's still tucked in the side of my bra. I can feel it laying here on my side."

"Awesome. We may get out of this yet." Marla wondered about her own phone. "Not sure where mine is."

"Me either," Mitzi said. "It's wherever my purse is."

Tick. Tick. Tick.

She twisted her right foot a little, trying to feel if her pistol was still in her ankle holster. Had they seen that? If she could eventually reach it....

Tick. Tick. Tick.

Soft moans came from her right, and Marla froze, staring that way. "Someone else is in here," she whispered, jerking harder at her restraints.

"Who?"

"I dunno!"

"Are we in a prison or something?"

"No clue, sis. Just keep working those hands."

Tick. Tick. Tick.

More moans. Heavy breathing.

"Who is there? What are you doing?"

"M... Mar..."

Molly whispered, "It's a man."

Panic immediately welled up inside of Marla. *A man?* Cooter? "Cooter! Is that you?" *Time is running out.*

"Mar...la."

Shit. Shit. Shit! She tugged her wrists, pulling and stretching the restraints until she'd wiggled out one hand. "I'm coming. Hold on!"

Tick. Tick. Tick.

Quickly, she got rid of the fabric binding her hands and checked her boot. Good. The ankle holster had slid down, and the gun was still there. By the looks of things, they were dealing with amateur kidnappers here—cloth restraints, and they didn't find her gun...or Molly's phone.

She patted her back jeans pockets. Her phone was gone.

"I'm out. Molly, say something so I can find you and your phone. Let's get a flashlight on things."

"I'm right here. You're in front of me. Phone's in my bra."

"Got it." Marla fumbled around Molly's shirt, found the phone, and flashed the light on her sisters. "Oh God, you two look lovely."

"I smell like hog slop on a steamy August afternoon. Get me loose."

"Turn around."

Tick. Tick. Tick.

Marla made quick work of freeing Molly, then Mitzi, and then flashed the light in the opposite direction.

"Cooter? Is that you?"

Tick. Tick.

Heavy breathing came from a lump over in the corner. Then, "Mar..."

"Oh, God." She pushed up, slipping on the damp floor a little, and rushed to the man. Her sisters padded along behind her. Getting there, she shined the light toward his face.

Tick.

There he was, her Cooter. Long hair, scruffy beard several days past scruff, his face was bloated and his eyes half-lidded.

"Darlin'," he squeaked out. "What...took you...so long?"

He appeared dazed and disoriented.

"Cooter. Oh, baby." Marla kneeled next to him and touched his face. "What the hell. Are you okay?"

He blinked. "Will be." Cooter's eyes focused on her, and he managed a weak smile. "That really you?"

"Yes, it's me," Marla replied, relief flooding through her. "What the hell happened?"

Cooter struggled with his words. "Accident. Can't remember much. Blur."

"You remember coming to me?"

A slight smile crossed his face. "Dream...."

Whatever it was, it didn't matter now. She'd found him.

And he was alive!

Marla's heart ached with happiness and also worry, but they had no time to dwell on either. "We need to find a way out of this dump."

"Not sure I can make it, darlin'."

She patted him down. His hands were bound too, and his feet. Quickly, she removed his restraints. Her sisters leaned over her shoulder.

"Oh God, Cooter. It's damn good to see you," Mitzi blurted out.

"Wish... I could see you. Blurry."

Marla flashed the light around the room, looking around for any sign of an exit. "We are going to get you out of here and to a medical facility." The room was small and cluttered, with wooden crates stacked against the walls. Could they move those and reach that window? Her brain spun. Was that a door on the far wall?

"Marla," Molly said, "Give me my phone. Let me text Brody. Maybe he can help us."

"Good idea." She handed the phone over to her sister.

Molly's fingers flew over her keyboard. "There. Told him we were kidnapped, the last place was Harry's, that maybe we're in a warehouse."

"Good."

Her phone pinged. Molly read the text. "He says he's five minutes away, and he's calling the cops. To hold on. Calvary is coming."

"If he finds us."

"Tell him to send an emergency squad." Marla kneeled beside Cooter. "Think you can you sit up? I'll help."

"May...be."

Marla pushed her left arm behind his back. "Lean on me, baby. I'll try to pull you closer."

It was a struggle, but with Mitzi's help, they got him into a sitting position.

He groaned, leaning into Marla. "My damn head. They drugged me with something. I remember a needle coming at me. And I think I broke my ankle in the bike wreck."

Marla didn't want to think about that. If the ankle was broken days ago, that didn't bode well for Cooter. Was he at risk of infection? Clots? Something else?

She didn't want to dwell on that. "You need food and water. Soon."

"I'm woozy as shit," he said.

Marla's heart hurt. "I'll take care of you, Cooter. I love you."

He rested his head against her shoulder. "Same."

Marla knew she wasn't going to get him into a standing position. "Girls, one or both of you has to go for help. We can't rely on Brody alone. Take the phone and find a way out. I'll stay here with Cooter. Just be careful you don't run into anyone."

"Oh no, we're not leaving you." Mitzi shook her head.

"No," said Molly.

"Look," Marla told them. "The best way for all of us to survive this is for at least one of you to go."

The sisters exchanged a glance.

"I'll do it," Mitzi said after a minute. "Give me the phone."

"No. I'm going with you." She turned to her older sister and Cooter. "You're sure you will be okay here?"

"Positive. I have my friend in my boot."

"Good."

"Check that door back there. See if you can get it open."

The two women headed that way.

Footsteps urgently sounded above them, followed by the slamming of a heavy door. The noise echoed through the empty structure above.

The girls halted, turning around to catch Marla's eye. "Please be Brody."

"Pray it's Brody," she whispered.

Marla's heart pounded against Cooter's shoulder. The cellar door creaked open, releasing a flood of light into the room from a hallway. A figure emerged, backlit by the light, and moved into the darker room.

Oh. My. God.

Marla gasped. "Luke?" At the moment, she wasn't sure if he was friend...or foe. "What the hell?"

"Damn. You." Cooter spit out.

Luke's expression was somewhat detached. "I'm sorry. I had to lie."

"I don't understand."

He looked directly at Marla. "I needed you three to come back down to music row tonight. I told you someone spotted Cooter, but that wasn't exactly the truth. They wanted you out of the picture and I thought if I could help make that happen, then they'd leave us all alone. Stay off our backs."

"You drugged us?"

Luke whirled toward Molly. "No. That wasn't me or my idea. I was simply going to find you and take you to Cooter."

"Why would you do that?" Marla asked, fearing her crackly voice revealed more emotion than she wanted. "So, you let them —whoever they are—stick us all down here in this godforsaken moldy hellhole to keep us safe? Naw. Not buying it."

Luke's eyes flickered with a mix of guilt and determination. "There are people who want Cooter silenced. Totally out of the picture, and they would do anything to ensure he doesn't talk. I was afraid the three of you were going to get tossed into the mix, too."

"Yet, isn't that what happened?"

"Yeah," he replied. "Sort of. Thing is, they think I'm on their side. I snuck away to see if I could get you all out of here."

Cooter stirred. "They want me dead. Right?"

Luke gazed at his friend. "They want you dead, and after tonight, probably me along with you."

Marla bit her lip, her gaze playing over Cooter. "What do you know?"

Cooter let out a lengthy sigh. "It's complicated darlin'."

"Give me the short version." She glared.

"Landry and I had a deal to keep his kid out of trouble," he said. "Guess he wanted to back out of it." He coughed hard, sputtering. "It had to do with the bar, not the band."

"I'm confused." Marla could see he was using all the energy he had just to sit up and talk. Suddenly felt bad for pressing him. "Luke, what is going on? What do you know?"

"It's Landry and his son, Jack. They both have loose screws in their heads. I was trying to save the bar. I might have lost it."

"Damn brother..." Cooter breathed the words.

"We need to get all of you out of here before they realize I am here."

"How?" Marla said. "There's no way Cooter can get up those steps."

"I know." He glanced about. "Maybe there is another way out."

Mitzi stepped closer, Molly on her heels. "I think Luke is right. We need to get out of here somehow. You three can sort this shit out later."

Molly grabbed her sister's arm. "But wait...."

The cellar door clanged back against the wall. Everyone shot their attention that way.

Shadows passed through the open space, catching Marla's eye. She nodded to her sisters in warning. As the two men approached, she inched her hand down her leg to reach her boot, and slowly drew out her pistol, tucking it into her hand.

Landry and another man—his son, Jack?—strode forward. "Yeah, we're fucking crazy. More than a few screws loose, I would say." They brushed by Mitzi and Molly, barely tossing them a glance as they headed toward Marla, Cooter, and Luke.

Obviously, they had been listening to their conversation.

"Sonofabitch," Cooter slurred.

"Better believe it." Landry moved closer. "Came to pick up some trash here. Gotta head off to the dump."

Out of the corner of her eye, she noticed Molly texting on her phone.

Marla stood, hoping to distract Landry. "Now, back off, dude. We're not going anywhere with you. In fact, I'm getting Cooter out of here right now. He needs medical attention."

Landry laughed. "Seriously? You and what army?"

She raised her arms, aimed her weapon, and took a stance. "Me, Smith, and Wesson here. Back up."

"Whoa," Molly hissed.

"That's my girl," Cooter murmured.

Landry cocked his head and sneered. "Or?"

"Or, which do you prefer, a bullet in your thigh or your foot? I don't want to kill you—unless I have too. But I'm not above incapacitating you for a while. Of course, if I shoot you in the thigh, I could hit an artery and you'd bleed out before anyone could get to you in this dingy bat cave. Or, I could miss entirely and take out the family jewels."

"Now hey there." Jack made a move toward her.

She swiveled her weapon, aiming toward his head. "Correction. I'll just take out this family jewel, although I don't think he's much of a gem."

Marla noticed Luke inching toward Cooter out of the corner of her eye, and that made her nervous. She kept her gaze directed at Landry. "Now, my sisters, they are going to leave, and you are going to let them."

Landry chuckled. "No. That's not how this is going to work."

Sirens abruptly wailed outside the cracked window, painting the dark room with flashes of red and blue.

Luke took advantage of the distraction to tackle Landry and pin him to the hard floor.

Jack bolted toward them, but Marla intervened, shoving her pistol in his back. "Don't move, sucker."

Brody's shouts echoed between the damp walls as he burst through the cellar door, his gun drawn, and running toward them.

There was no time for anyone else to react. Law enforcement swarmed in behind Brody, their guns drawn as well. Their presence flooded Marla with relief and a sense of finality. She lowered her gun and stuck it in her boot.

The officers wasted no time cuffing Luke, Landry, and Jack.

She turned her gaze on Luke. "I don't get you."

"Marla, please," he whispered, his eyes pleading. "Let me explain."

But she turned away, unwilling to meet him even halfway. She was still very confused about Luke's involvement. She had trusted him. Had he played her?

"It won't help." She went to Cooter.

He coughed the words. "He'll... come... around."

"I'm not sure I will." Her stomach hurt just saying that out loud.

Brody interrupted. "Luke definitely has some explaining to do, but let's not jump to conclusions." Crouching before Cooter, he added, "EMS is in the alley. They'll be down to get you soon and get you to the hospital." He glanced up. "You girls, too. You should get checked out."

"I, for one, can't wait to get out of the damp cavern that smells like pee," Mitzi said.

"Me, for two," Molly added. "Couldn't have done it without you, Brody." She looked at him in adoration.

Marla was grateful for Brody's timely arrival. "Seriously, thank you," she told him.

Brody snickered, glancing from one sister to another. "Oh, I'm pretty sure the three of you would have given Rick and Jack a run for their money."

Cooter spit out a chuckle. "I guaran-damn-tee it!"

Chapter Ten

"How is he?"

Marla looked up from Cooter's hospital bed, where she had obviously slept awkwardly hunched over the side, while both her sisters moved into the small room. How long had she slept like that? No wonder her neck hurt.

"So much better," she told them, yawning, and sitting up straighter. "The nurses cleaned him up and got him some food and water. He was cracking jokes."

"That's awesome news!"

"Yeah."

"They took him about twenty minutes ago—to an orthopedic surgeon to look at the ankle."

The sisters moved closer. Mitzi gave Marla a hug. "Did he tell you anything about the accident?"

Nodding, Marla stared off, remembering the conversation she and Cooter had earlier. "Yes. He went off all half-cocked on his bike after Jack, not Landry. I guess after he and Landry tussled on stage, Jack cold-cocked him outside and took off. Before he realized it, he'd chased him into Texas on highway 31, heading toward Killeen. Of course, they didn't get that far."

"The accident?"

"Yes." Marla shuddered, thinking about Cooter getting hurt. "Jack evidently pulled off and hid at the side of the road somewhere. Cooter passed him, then when Jack caught up, he tried to run him off the road. Their bikes got tangled up and both of them went skidding off into the ravine. That's when Cooter broke his ankle."

"Oh geez. How awful." Molly grimaced.

Mitzi frowned. "That had to hurt like a mother."

"He said it was so painful he passed out for a while. When he woke up, it was raining. Jack and his bike were gone, and someone was carrying him away from the accident scene. That's when they gave him a sedative, we think. Which may have been a blessing because of the ankle. The next thing he remembers was the cellar, and he was in and out of consciousness for those few days."

"Wow."

"Did they feed him and give him water?"

"Some, yes." Marla scowled.

"That's all very scary."

Marla looked her sisters over. "Yeah. How are you two?"

"We're fine." Molly leaned against the bed.

Mitzi sat in a chair behind Marla. "You need to get checked out by the doctor. We'll wait here."

"I'll go with you," Molly said.

She pushed back and studied her sisters. "What did the doctor say about the drugs in our drinks?"

"They took blood and urine tests. Might be one of those date rape drugs."

"Great." She stood. "I don't suppose my blood or urine would make a difference then. Whatever goes for the two of you likely goes for me, too. Did they talk about side effects?"

Molly nodded. "Headaches, disorientation, vomiting maybe,

depending on how much we ingested. Since we weren't out for long, they think the side effects could be minor. We might have a bit of amnesia around the time it all happened."

Marla thought about that. "You know, I don't remember much. After we left the pool hall, my mind is a blank slate."

"We don't either."

"I wish I could remember who attacked us." In the back of her mind, she wondered if Luke really was involved.

Molly fiddled with the edge of the blanket. "All I remember is the sensation of falling, then waking up with my face on the cold floor."

Marla nodded. "That's about it for me, too."

A few seconds of silence passed, then Mitzi asked, "Anything from Luke?"

Pushing away from the bed, Marla paced a few steps toward the window, staring out onto the streetlight lit parking lot, dawn breaking slowly across the way, behind the trees. "Nothing. I don't expect to hear from him. I'm just so disappointed."

Molly approached and laid her head on her big sister's shoulder. "There's a lot we don't know. Don't get worked up over it yet."

"I know." Marla was just sad, though. She'd thought Luke a friend and now she wasn't so sure. And how would this affect Cooter? She knew he trusted Luke, too.

They both turned as Brody pushed into the room. "And there they are, all three Newberry girls in one place." He moved to Molly, gave her a kiss on the cheek, and pulled her to his side. "You okay?"

She nodded. "I'm fine."

"I'm sorry I couldn't stay. They wanted me at the station to get a statement and ask some questions. They are going to want to talk to the three of you, too."

Molly leaned into his embrace. "It's fine. I'm just glad you were close and that you could get there quickly. The police too."

"It helped that we'd put the 360 app on our phones the other day. Remember? So we could keep track of each other? At first I thought that was overkill, but now I'm a fan. The app led me straight to you."

Molly's smile stretched wide. "Oh, I forgot about that!"

Marla watched the intensity of the look passing between her sister and Brody. The girl sure looked like she was in love. She hoped Brody wouldn't break her heart. Molly had had enough hurt for a lifetime in the love department.

"So, what about Luke, Brody? Any news about what's going on with him?"

"I saw him earlier down at the station. He's detained, still had to be processed so—"

Footsteps halted at the hospital room door, stopping Brody's words. Marla turned and looked that way.

Luke.

* * *

"What are you doing here?"

She knew she shouldn't be so angry with him and wasn't sure why it was all bubbling up inside her now. Probably because she hated being taken advantage of or lied to. She sure hoped Luke hadn't done either.

"I can tell you everything you need to know," he said, focusing on her.

"They let you go?" Brody asked.

"They did. Landry and Jack confessed to everything. And I don't mind saying I'm rather relieved because I didn't like keeping things from any of you." His gaze suddenly became more intense. "Especially you and Cooter, Marla."

"Well then," came the voice from the door. "You can start fessing up any time now. Looks like the gang's all here."

A nursing assistant wheeled Cooter into the room. Cooter gave Luke a stare while passing.

Everyone else shifted their attention, too. Marla crossed the room and leaned in to give her guy a kiss on the cheek. "You're back."

"Yes," he said, smiling up at her. "Surgery at one, they say."

"Today?" That surprised her.

Cooter nodded. "Been too long since the break. He wants to get it done. I said to have at it."

"Goodness. Okay." Marla exhaled, hard. *One more thing...*

The assistant angled the wheelchair closer to the bed. "Let's get him settled," he said, nodding toward the door.

Cooter's nurse joined them. Looking at him directly, she said, "Doctor ordered rest, so say goodbyes for now. This crew will need to leave."

Cooter spanned the room, looking first at Marla, then her sisters and Brody, and lingering on Luke. "Before they go, we need to clear the air about a few things."

"Can you make it quick?" The nurse narrowed her eyes.

"Maybe." He chuckled.

"I'll rephrase," the nurse said. "Make it quick."

"All right. All right." He snorted and gave her a wave of defeat.

Marla angle closer, her gaze fixed on Cooter. "I think there are some things you need to tell me." She gave him a saucy grin. "Are you avoiding that?"

He shook his head and grasped her hand. "No. Come here." Tucking her hand inside his, he tugged her closer to sit next to him, then studied the group around his bed.

"Look. We caught Jack Landry stealing money out of my office at the bar one night after a late set, a few months ago. The kid was on probation in California for doing basically the same thing. I told Landry I would keep it under wraps as long as the kid paid me back."

"Was it a lot of money?"

"Ten thousand dollars. It was all caught on the surveillance camera in my office. Luke left the safe cracked open when he put the night deposit in. Unintentionally, of course."

Luke moved closer to Cooter. "I've felt guilty as hell about it ever since. Totally my fault. I was in a hurry with the deposits for the night and didn't get the damn thing closed."

"And he's been trying to make up for it ever since."

Marla studied Luke. "How?"

"By getting chummy with Landry. Trying to get on his good side, so we could see what else he was up to."

Cooter continued. "I should have called the police but handled it directly with Landry. I had taken a loan from Landry a few years ago when I bought the bar and was paying him back as we had agreed—but out of the blue Landry called in the balance. I told him I couldn't do that, and he got pissed."

Marla thought about the cash receipts she'd seen in the safe. "So he was threatening to take the bar?"

"Yes, but he didn't have a leg to stand on." Cooter glanced at Luke. "Still, I had a sneaking suspicion Landry was up to no good, so I wanted to keep him close, not push him away. I could have gotten Jack into a lot of additional trouble, so I used that to hold over Landry's head. We planned for him to deposit the money Jack owed into a temporary account, a thousand dollars a month, which would then be directly deposited into my account. I didn't want to deal with cash on this. I wanted a record."

"Oh! The mystery deposits in your account!" When Cooter's brow arched, she added, "We went through your accounts and stuff, Luke and I, trying to find clues."

He laughed. "Of course you did. You thought I was dead."

"I was trying to find motive, answers."

"And eventually you did."

She stared into his eyes. "I wasn't going to stop, Cooter. I never would have stopped."

They shared a deep gaze for several seconds.

"If I could add to this," Luke interjected. "About last night... I had to buddy up with Landry so I could figure out where Cooter was, make sure he was safe, and get him home. And then also when you three came up missing. I told him you were going to be at Harry's last night, and I'm responsible for that." His gaze scanned the three women. "I'm sorry. I didn't know they were going to drug you. The plan was to scare you enough that you'd stop going around town and asking questions. That's why I set out to find you as soon as possible."

Marla interrupted him. "Then why didn't you just tell us to lay off, not go to music row anymore and dig up dirt?"

Luke laughed. "Like me telling you not to go would stop you?"

She looked at her sisters, who both shrugged. "Be honest with yourself, Marla," Mitzi said.

She shook off her words, then looked at Luke. "Of course, that wouldn't have stopped us."

"I rest my case."

Marla exhaled. "I don't know if it's the aftereffect of the drugs or if all of this just makes my head spin too much."

"Probably both."

The nurse stepped into the group. "Are you about to wrap up here?"

Cooter raised a finger. "One more minute."

She nodded, sighed, and stepped away again.

Luke continued. "The law got a full confession out of Landry. He and Jack never planned to pay back the full amount they owed you, Cooter. If you were out of the picture, then Landry felt he was clear. But there is more."

"Of course." Marla laughed nervously. "There's always more..."

Cooter squeezed her hand. "You're right. You see? Landry and me, we've had a long-standing rivalry. He enjoyed having me in the band because I was a draw, but he didn't enjoy paying me my rate. We haggled about it for years, but he always gave it up. I think he may have seen an opportunity to assert some kind of control. But...."

"But then Jack Landry slipped into the picture," Luke said. "Landry's son was jealous of Cooter's talent and popularity. He believed that by getting rid of Cooter, he will become the star of the music scene around here, and finally receive the recognition he craved and deserved."

"Wait." Marla held Luke's gaze. Something was missing. "You knew Jack Landry was the rival drummer? You never said a word the night we discussed."

Luke nodded. "I know. I didn't want that known right then. Landry needed to keep an eye on his son, I think. Keep him close and hopefully out of trouble. Of course, if Cooter was out of the band, then he didn't have to pay him the higher wage, too. So, that killed two birds, one stone."

"And then there is the complication of the bar itself," Cooter added.

Molly leaned in, then glanced at Marla. "Didn't Landry say something about 'time and technicality' in getting the bar for himself?"

Nodding, Marla agreed. "He did. What did that mean, Cooter?"

"Here's the deal. I wanted to make Landry a partner in the bar back in the day when I was just opening up. He laughed and said the place wasn't going to go anywhere. Good luck with

110

that. The location was poor, and he said I'd never get gigs or people to drive all the way out there. But he was wrong. Instead, he bought a bar downtown that flopped. He kept trying and eventually, he sort of became king over the downtown scene, but he could never top what I was doing at my place."

"Yeah," Luke said. "Cooter's bar become one of the most popular spots for local bands and musicians in the area, and even beyond, which threatened Landry's control locally. Control he desperately wanted to keep."

"Landry's ego was bruised somewhat. Both he and his son have extreme issues with that shit." Cooter squeezed Marla's hand. She could tell he was getting tired.

"So," she began, "Landry and Jack wanted to eliminate the competition, you, and monopolize the music scene around here? And getting rid of Cooter was the fastest way to do that. Plus, it kept his son out of trouble, and they got to keep the money."

Cooter nodded. "Apparently. And with me gone, he figured he'd acquire the bar property and expand their music empire."

Luke nodded. "Evidently he'd drawn up some sort of fake paperwork saying he was part owner of the bar, and that your half came to him upon your death."

Cooter blew out a long breath. "Wow." He coughed a few times, then lay back on his pillow.

"All right." The nurse wiggled her way into the group again. "Time to leave for a while." She waved them out.

Everyone but Marla shuffled out of the room. She held back, waiting for the hospital staff to check Cooter's vital signs and leave.

After the assistant left, she leaned in and kissed him square on the lips and whispered. "I don't ever want to be away from you again. I hope you are ready for that."

He grinned through his scraggly, scruffy beard. "More than ready, darlin'."

"Then scoot over." She kicked off her shoes, climbed into bed and nuzzled close into the crook of his shoulder. He wrapped an arm around her upper body.

The nurse moved to the foot of the bed, smiling. "Everything okay here?"

"Perfect," Marla murmured, then sat up a little, tugging at the blanket. "Oh, those people out there in the hallway? Send them away, please, and tell them not to come back until after five o'clock this evening."

She met the nurse's gaze head on, and the young woman nodded. "Of course. He needs his sleep."

Marla yawned. "And not a minute before."

"Absolutely." She headed for the door.

"No, wait."

The nurse turned back.

"Tell them not to come until tomorrow."

* * *

A few hours later, Marla blinked awake from a heavy sleep. She wondered if the drugs were still in her system. The lights were off in the room, the blinds closed on the windows, and the curtain drawn around the bed. Goodness, she didn't remember any of that happening.

Snorting a little, she shifted, glancing at the bedside clock. It wasn't yet ten o'clock.

"You're drooling on my pretty hospital gown," Cooter said.

"Lovely." She sat up, swiping at her mouth, and smiled. "Hey."

"Hey you," he whispered. "I wonder if I get lunch before surgery."

"I'm betting not."

Cooter smirked. "Was afraid of that."

"I'm just glad there are no complications with the ankle."

"Yes. Me, too."

Her gaze played over his face. "Cooter?"

"Yes, my love?"

"Did you have dreams when you were out?"

He grinned. "I was with you every minute, darlin'."

Marla felt tears stinging her eyes. "You came to me," she whispered.

He tugged her closer. "I will always come to you."

She angled in for a slow, lazy kiss. "Will your ankle be healed by summer?"

"I sure as hell hope so, darlin'. I have plans."

"Oh?

He nodded, leaning his head back against his pillow. "Yes. You, me, and the Harley. An open road in front of us, and the Dead in our ear buds."

Marla cuddled close into his chest and sighed. Nothing had ever sounded so perfect. "I can't wait," she whispered.

"Me, either, my love."

Do you get Maddie's VIP Insider News?

Be the first to get the latest news about my books—new releases, free ebooks, sales and discounts, sneak peeks, and exclusive content! Just add your email address at this link: https://maddiejamesbooks.com/pages/newsletter

Whether writing flirty contemporary romance or gritty romantic suspense, Maddie James writes to silence the people in her head.

In 2022, Maddie celebrated her 25th year of publishing romance fiction under multiple pen names. Her collective body of work includes over 70 titles. Maddie loves writing small town contemporary romance and cowboy worlds, and as M.L. Jameson she pens romantic suspense.

Affair de Coeur says Maddie, "shows a special talent for traditional romance," and RT Book Reviews claimed, "James deftly combines romance and suspense, so hop on for an exhilarating ride."

Do you get Maddie's VIP Insider News?

Learn more and buy books direct at www. maddiejamesbooks.com.

Milton Keynes UK
Ingram Content Group UK Ltd.
UKHW040653050923
428087UK00004B/459

9 781622 375516